Praise for A Virtual Image

Rosalind Brackenbury has an exciting story to tell in *A Virtual Image*…. she tells it with conspicuous success. This intelligent and satisfying second novel confirms the good opinions that she won with *A Day to Remember to Forget*.

Francis King, The Sunday Telegraph

The excitement of the search for the mysterious Anna is paralleled by the revelation of the relationship between the two girls, stretching back into childhood. Excellently written, a very satisfying second novel.

The Times

With a painting holiday in view, Ruby journeys through France to the Camargue in search of her friend Anna. The latter proves increasingly mysterious and illusive, and the quest takes on a deeper significance, not without its bizarre encounters. Splendidly written and very gripping.

The Sunday Times

A journey of self-discovery as much as of search. On the surface the story, with its brief series of encounters, and its charming landscapes, is an extremely simple one, but it also manages to convey a real sense of a character trying to peer beneath her experiences into the depth of her identity.

Donald McCormick, The Glasgow Herald

A VIRTUAL IMAGE

A VIRTUAL IMAGE

by

ROSALIND BRACKENBURY

introduced by

JANET BURROWAY

SANDNESS
MICHAEL WALMER
2020

ERRATUM
This edition has been created utilizing a previous edition; thus an error
has been reproduced. On page 45, line 17, for *is is?*, please read *is it?*

INTRODUCTION

Two girls, thrown together by the proximity of their childhood homes, develop a life-long relationship. Are they friends? One would certainly say so. As children they play together contentedly enough, each cocooned in her own imagination. As adolescents they both have "the dreams from which one awakens half-ashamed" and compete for the attention of boys as adolescent girls will. The narrator tells us, "there was nobody to whom I was closer," but "in the real sense we were never called upon to meet," and the trope will take on a tense reality.

As the novel begins these two young women, in their late twenties, have a plan to meander through southern France, Anna to go on ahead, her friend to meet her on the way. Anna has become tall, blonde, willowy, with a tendency to "the silence of sweet reasonableness." Her friend is dark, short, square; she "can talk and make jokes." In spite of the clarity and realism of the narrative, it's impossible to miss the scent of fairy tale, of quest and test, of a bear who might be a prince—and to see the two as Snow White and Rose Red, for the shorter of the young women is named Ruby.

Ruby is our eyes and ears for nearly all of the novel, a perceptive and eloquent narrator who consistently, as in the descriptions above, puts herself down. She claims, "I lived inside my swarthiness and plumpness and watched the growth of [Anna's] fair cool beauty without surprise, as one might watch a tree." She says, "People just think I'm half-caste or something." She says, "I only teach art," but, "she's a painter." When Anna declares, "God, the open road, I can hardly wait. It's the only thing that really makes me feel free," Ruby readily acquiesces, before she knows whether this is what she feels or not. In the event, the open road can make her feel by turns freedom or fear. Lonely on the long drive, she perceives a mutual dependence: "Together, it seems, we know who we individually are."

Ruby and Anna have made an itinerary of sorts for their journey, a casual series of towns, friends, projects, they can explore together. But as the novel goes on, Anna becomes increasingly elusive and Ruby increasingly anxious in pursuit, with "the beginning of the fear that I had been excluded." Anna, for example, was to make a stop with Ruby's friends Howard and Jeannie, who as it turns out, however, were away. Weren't they? Their friend Caley, the "roughneck" American poet, would have been there, wouldn't he? He and Anna might have finished off all the wine in the house, perhaps? The only real clue is a toothpaste tube on the bathroom floor.

Similarly at the artists' retreat where Ruby and Anna had agreed to paint together: had Anna arrived? It seems so, until the "bit of an ice maiden" who has been mistaken for her shows up and proves to be an entirely different person. At each stage of the journey the stakes increase with the mystery, for when Ruby crosses paths with the roughneck poet, it turns out that he is in pursuit of Anna as well.

A Virtual Image was Rosalind Brackenbury's second novel, but published in 1971, the same year as her first, *A Day to Remember to Forget*. The first-published book explored, through the consciousness of four characters, ambivalence toward marriage. *A Virtual Image* explores ambivalence toward friendship; and these two themes resonate throughout Brackenbury's remarkable and prolific life as a novelist and poet. Indeed, the pursuit of an elusive friend through France recurs in her most recent, seventeenth, novel *Without Her,* though this story has a different significance and a different denouement. One can see both the strong and nimble talent of an original in the earlier story and the sure hand and acquired wisdom of the later.

But *A Virtual Image* of itself presents us with a born storyteller and a stylist. Brackenbury has a command of rising suspense and of gorgeous images: "the blond cows slowly passing down a lane," "the sun coming through the curtains like orange juice," "a piece of shore that is ashen, like the surface of the moon, where trees that have been twisted in the sea lie beached, and pyramids of salt cut geometry into the sky." She is particularly good at writing about the body and sexual pleasure, equally adept at staying with a thought, worrying it until it yields up an insight that will propel the narrative.

I have said that the story is told almost entirely from Ruby's point of view. Almost, but not quite. At widely spaced intervals we get, first, a scrap of dialogue that certainly takes place where she is not, and then passages told from either Anna's vantage point or Caley's, as if the narrative must veer off course in order to give us the full story.

Is this necessary? Wouldn't it have been possible to let Ruby speculate, or invent some other character or characters to fill in the missing information? Is it a beginner's choice to leap from one viewpoint to another when it suits the author's needs?

Brackenbury relates that at some point a reader suggested Anna does not really exist, and was a figment of Ruby's imagination, a part of herself that she needed to deal with or destroy. Even the jacket flap of the original publication suggests that "The image which draws her always on may be an illusion." But the author has said that this was not her intention at all. Anna exists.

Why then diverge from Ruby's perception to fill in the narrative blanks?

I am going to suggest that it is not the author but Ruby herself who invents these passages. At one point she says, "In my effort to assimilate what is happening, I hold imaginary conversations," and proceeds to do so, until she is held back by reluctance because she has encountered "a part of my picture of myself…a delicate thing" she does not want to put into words. "And yet I see what is happening. It is strong, clear in my mind….And so I try again."

Perhaps she does. In a passage soon after Ruby and Caley meet, the narrating Caley thinks, 'You fall in love with a type, made for your own destruction…to cast yourself fatally into her." He laments:

> I have to entangle myself with a thoughtless English bitch in the middle of France; I have to be fool enough to hunt for her when she is gone and so find upon my trail her friend, the ugly and intelligent one of the two, I imagine, the one with all of the imagination and none of the self-confidence.

Is this Caley's perspective or Ruby's? It certainly comes close to expressing both her frustration with Anna at this point and her incipient jealousy as she and Caley begin a dance of advance and retreat. "The ugly and intelligent one" suggests rather Ruby's habitual self-put-down than the opinion of a man whose sexual interest is clearly piqued by her.

Later, there is an extended, sensitive and empathetic scene in which Anna readies herself for the painting of a landscape. But the time of the telling of this part of the story comes much later, when Ruby has the facts at her command and has had time to put them into loving perspective, when it is perhaps she who steps in to paint in words the picture that Anna has not.

These are speculations on my part. I offer them because the layers of meaning in this early but assured novel invite and repay such speculation. But there is one clue to Brackenbury's method in the text itself. The title *A Virtual Image* may seem to be a tautology, since in literary terms an image is always virtual, implying something that is not there, and the virtual is by definition not material.

This is, however, not the case in the science of optics, where an image is defined as the collection of focus points of light rays coming from an object. A real image is the collection of focus points actually made by converging rays, while a virtual image is the collection of focus points made by extensions of diverging rays, using a diverging lens or a convex mirror. The light rays appear to emanate from the virtual image but do not actually exist at the position of that virtual image. Thus is holography made, where we can see people appearing fully present, who seem to move and speak though they are not there. At the end of *A Virtual Image*, the author has appended a discrete note:

> In holography an object can be created visually, by the use of a laser beam. Each minute portion of the holographic plate contains the whole image. In a pure light any virtual image can be recreated, in the position in which it was originally seen.

This is a perfect metaphor for Anna, who is never there but perpetually present, exactly represented in her absence, determining the story, the thoughts and actions of the other characters from whom she has detached and disappeared. It is also consistent with the notion that Ruby empathetically creates the images of the other characters, the narrator as a laser beam using a convex mirror.

A Day to Remember to Forget assembles a vision of conventional married life that is universal and also particular to a moment in history, when women began to question the point of their domestic sacrifice. *A Virtual Image* explores the alternative situation of the same historical period, in which young women can newly, easily, travel alone, and must therefore learn to negotiate the dangers and frustrations of freedom. It offers a vivid portrait of our universal habit of comparing ourselves to others. And it creates for us a heroine in the hot chaos of discovering her true self.

JANET BURROWAY

Chicago, October 2020.

I see us at first as the two children somebody photographed one afternoon in the summer holidays; the
sun shone for a moment, an aunt of mine wanted to
finish up her film, the Box Brownie came out and we
faced it, giggling, shy, ten-year-olds caught and
made to turn from our private game, unable yet to
summon any confidence to meet the adult world. Our
parents lived next door to each other in those early
days, we were sent to the same school; and so it was
natural that in our intense and private fantasy worlds
we should come to face each other, to play opposite
each other in our ritual self-absorbed games, to

endow each other, momentarily, with the attributes each needed for the dramatic tension to be held. I forget what game we played, that afternoon – it could have been the one in which we were orphans in an orphanage, each to ourselves Jane Eyre, each thus allowing the other to be; it could have been Robin Hood, in which we were both, secretly, the nimble hero of the woods – but I remember the shock of an adult arriving in our hiding place, the disgraceful intrusion of the command, 'Smile, children!' and the furtive longing on that young aunt's face, to know what it was we did. We turned, grimaced; I saw the picture in later days and thought of monkeys, smiling with fear as they are let out of the capsules that have carried them through space; she, my friend, managed it better than I, for her features were malleable, she assumed easily the innocent mask of childhood and smiled out with equanimity from behind her blowing hair, giving away nothing, while I, a metal band holding in my teeth, a smear of mud upon one cheek, had simply turned and snarled my apprehension. 'What was it you were playing, darlings?' my Aunt Kathleen had asked, leaning against a tree-trunk in her unease, her long flowery skirt wrapping itself around her legs; and this time we both turned away, giggling, blushing, scuffing with our feet in the soft peaty earth, unable to reply. Questions held us immobile, wriggling like worms upon a pin; by the dire, questing accuracy of the adult world we were silenced and appalled. Anna had a rhyme; as the aunt turned to go, she began to mutter, in an incantation of self-defence, 'Silly old hag, silly old hag, stuff your head in a shopping-bag, silly old hag, silly old . . .' but I was already away again, a prisoner, perhaps, a suffering hero, a charity child in a school that would have interested de Sade, and I hardly heard her. I held my face averted, I scanned the miles of sea from my desert island, I sat, proudly musing, in my rat-infested cell; and then, as for so many times, so many hours with Anna, I was free. For she never made the demands, then, that one person makes upon another, she never wanted me to do anything, or stop doing anything, or descend to a prosaic level of truth; she, like me, was a child, enthroned in a solipsist world; and if to me a certain bush became a ship at sea, to her it could be equally a castle to be besieged. We were awakened, we were threatened, only by the presence of an uncomprehending third person, to whose eyes all that we did might seem insane. And whether this was natural or unnatural, normal or extraordinary, I still cannot say – for one's past, one's childhood is a landscape in which the dimly lifting rocks could jut in no other formation, the rivers flow in no other way. I only believe now that when one makes a deep and passionate pact with somebody to exclude all outer reality, there is danger that stirs beneath the safeness, a demand for an answer, a decision, that must one day be given. But in those days I lived in the glassy tower of my own preoccupations, meeting nobody who had not strayed out of novels or films; and when I looked up, to glance in my abstracted way to see if the world went on, I saw only Anna's face, as in a mirror, as if that was what I looked like to the strange outside, Anna's face, pale, set, equally enthralled, and I suppose when she glanced up, during those long holiday hours, what she saw was me. In codes, in private languages, in the phraseology of the books we read, we conversed with each other, sending messages. But in the real sense – if there is a meeting in a real sense – we were never called upon to meet. And there was nobody to whom I was closer than to her.

There are other photographs, other images, most of them suggesting nothing except time and place, a school concert, a picnic, a gymkhana somewhere, pictures in which the very clothes we wore and the accidental people in the background 'Old So-and-so, do you remember her . . . ?' would be enough to arouse nostalgia, but which, nevertheless, told nothing about our real, our hidden selves; for the quality of brutal awakening which that aunt of mine had unwittingly produced was ever afterwards missing. One becomes warier, perhaps, one guards against the sudden intrusion and no longer turns, instinctively, eyes candid and mouth for a moment defenceless, to see what it is that moves. The fantasy, the other life, becomes weighted down, buried beneath the falling sand of what is expected, so that it fumbles slower, dumb and snouting like a mole. The mounds thrown up are the poems and paintings of adolescence, the dreams from which one awakens half-ashamed, the impulses which, of course, one must not obey. And so, in these later pictures, we are ordinary school-girls, very ordinary, and have apparently forgotten what we once knew, or at least will never think of it again. After this, I am alone, and sometimes there is a dim pain, a groping after something I once nearly understood; but it hardly matters.

Twenty years after that uneasy photograph was

taken, I see myself as if from the outside, for I have been sitting still so long that I know now what I look like. Besides, I have been often told. I find myself at a particular point in time which seems important, a woman sitting in a flood of summer sunshine, beside a window. Dust dances in the light; and there is dust on the kitchen shelves, dust on the pots and pans and on the window pane, a blurred scene beyond the panes of summer London and the dried trees in the little park. Before me a cup of coffee stands on a folded newspaper, steam rising. Beside it there is a plate, dotted with black crumbs, a piece of toast and butter that smells like tin, with a bite out of it. There is the kettle, the milk bottle, the torn brown envelope with the electricity bill inside, a book from the library face downwards upon a chair, a pair of tights like thin bleached legs, dangling from the chair back, underwear soaking in a round red bowl in the sink. It is a room like thousands of other rooms, a room to camp in, to light fires in and leave easily, as nomads do. It is private and nobody comes in, its walls and floors buried under the organic growth, the tendrils of the person who lives there, putting out shoots, meeting the blank surfaces of loneliness. There are pictures, and a calendar. The calendar says that is the tenth of August, and the newspaper confirms it. Yet outside, in the heat, in the dryness, in the slow burning metal of traffic and the moving crowds, every day is much the same. I hold a postcard, I am re-reading it, turning it round now to examine the photograph on the front, turning it again to impose some form, some meaning, upon the words that were written nearly a week ago upon its back. I am holding a piece of a foreign country, a piece of France, which could yet have come from anywhere. In black and white, a field, a far house, a wooded hill; the house, it said, was a château, but it was hard to see. Why not have sent something definite, a famous view, something easily identified, evidently French? There is no point in sending photographs of obscure pieces of countryside. Neither, I am thinking, is there much point in sending messages that nobody can understand. 'Put it on a postcard,' people say, when they want to know something definite; make it succinct, make it clear. But Anna always sends this sort of message, presuming upon a telepathy that does not always function; one can never really tell whether she is enjoying herself, or well, or wanting to see one; for instead of any direct human announcement, there are these quotations, these private jokes, so that one has to search through books of poetry or fumble in one's memory for the allusion. This card of mine reads 'Luxe, calme et volupté? Give me Margate. S.U.S. A.' The postmark, somewhere unknown, a small town upon the Loire, perhaps. She posted it on her way south, and it has taken nearly a week. It has travelled across France, meaninglessly, for a week, and now it is here and will tell me nothing. Baudelaire, or was it Verlaine? And Margate is where Anna's parents now live. And See You Soon, her childish, hopeful abbreviation. I have put the card down on the table and am fingering its matt surface, ironing out the creases at the corners. It is the sort of very old, fingered postcard that one finds in shops where few tourists ever stop, one of a collection to be brought out from under the counter in a wooden box,

10

to be picked over. I look up from it to my square picture of sky, roofs, trees and television aerials, my well-known, well-watched piece of London. How may I conjure, from this piece of card, the presence of Anna in France? How find in it a direction that I am truly to go and meet her, as we have arranged? The smell of French cigarettes, the painted women on calendars, the half-empty bottles of Pernod and Ricard in the bars, a fat man in a beret on a bicycle; I range through my memories of France, the ones that everybody has, the common heritage; I try to recreate it, to see and smell and apprehend it, so that it may seem to have something to do with me, something mine in particular. In my mind I pursue distances down long avenues of plane-trees, soaring to the horizon, but it is useless, the essence evades me, the image is not mine alone. There is now only the next thing to do, and the one after that and the one after that, until finally I am there, finding my own reality and freed from nostalgia. And then Anna and I, there together, will laugh at the story behind the postcard, the ludicrous holiday incident, the joke that can be told and told again to others, once we are home and all has become clear.

I was always conscious, when I was with Anna, of my extreme darkness. Squat as a child, square still as an adult, with my brown skin and black hair and eyes, I was the 'coal-black smith' of the song, the dark lady, the villainess. How else could one interpret it? Anna, with her fine fair hair and the pallor of her oval face and the white skin that stretched blamelessly all over her with never a spot or blemish or sunburn rash, she even at fourteen was the virgin of all fairy tales. I lived inside my swarthiness and plumpness and watched the growth of her fair cool beauty without surprise, as one might watch a tree. I see us, the black and the golden, growing older, beginning in our teens to exchange glances less lucid than those of childhood, as the hunt begins and boys become a quarry too precious to be lost to any friendship with a girl. I see the hostile glances become conspiratorial, as we realise that together we are better equipped than singly, that black Ruby can talk and make jokes, while pale Anna smiles distantly, and calculates, and dangles a little silver bag from her wrist, looking down. I, Ruby Smith, how could I be otherwise, with my blacksmith's dusty heritage, my ancestors that murmured to horses and twisted molten iron and seared·with their red-hot instruments into the burning hoof? How could I not have found my opposite, my foil, in a pale child with the features of a fairy, the silence of sweet reasonableness, the hidden will of a goddess? For I was changeable and moody, a genius with jokes and stories, they said, a clown with the clown's weight to bear, the melancholy soul behind the mask. And she, who was called Anna, Anna Parrish, a name full of light and cleanliness that was to be found inscribed everywhere beside my own, she somehow needed to be followed and encouraged and entertained. With you as clown, she seemed to be saying, how can I help but be the princess? And so we helped, we supported each other, as life became an affair of surface complications. As we grew older, the wary, witty, mutual friendliness set into a kind of cast; we defined each

12

other, each by our presence acting to the company the show it expected to see. Two halves of a turn. I see our eyes meet past some man's indecision, in perfect complicity, and see a decision made. We were arrogant, we were false. In retrospect, I think she was slightly less wicked, because more innocent, than I.

It was her idea, going to France, her idea that a summer school for painting somewhere in the wooded hills of the Lot valley should be our holiday base that year; she who wished perhaps for a return to the kind of holiday we had taken as students, I who remarked cruelly that at twenty-seven one could hardly hitch-hike about the country eating bread and cheese and staying in youth hostels without inviting ridicule; she finally who had mentioned this couple, this middle-aged ménage in south-western France to whom we could go in all respectability. Neither of us, I think, said aloud or even admitted consciously that this would do very well as a useful cover for whatever else we found to do. For we both paint, Anna rather well, I well enough to enjoy it and to teach art in a secondary school in London. It seemed a perfectly good idea. We wrote to Thomas and Kirstin Fairbrother and they wrote back. They were expecting us. It was all arranged.

Anna, said, 'Of course, it may be dreadfully dreary.'

'But it might be marvellous,' I said.

'Well, I suppose there's always France. There's always the wine and the sun and the peaches dropping off the trees and all those lovely cheap ciggies and the romantic French.' She spoke lightly, and I knew that we both imagined the same thing.

I said, 'What about Ian?'

'Ian? Oh, very, very finished, I'm afraid. Didn't I tell you? We had endless rows, from about last Christmas.' I did not ask her why, fearing to see in her explanation the mirrored image of my own situation. But she, careless at the time, asked me 'What about your beautiful violin maker? John, wasn't it? The one with the purple trousers.' I accepted the blow; it was fair, I suppose, and since we had agreed to go on holiday together, for the first time for years, without men, there had to be some basic explanations. I said, 'He got married. To a lady from Clapham.'

'Clapham? How very unfortunate!' and she began to laugh, picking out at once the bawdy and absurd from the most ordinary event, until I laughed with her and was almost set free.

'Still,' she said, sober again, 'he should have married you, lovely Ruby. The boorish beast.'

And I said blindly, 'Oh, no, that'd never have done.'

And so she, who had sold a painting, went on in advance to look at Brittany on the way, while I, who had bought a new stereo, an apricot silk dress and four new tyres for my car, typed other people's theses and planned to follow her. My other friends were all out of London; alone in my room, with the crisp pages of typescript piling up next door, and the dust, and the crumbs, and the sooty pigeons, and London outside burnished like a new coin in the ceaseless sun, I waited for it to be time to leave. Anna sent me this postcard from somewhere on the Loire; she must

14

be on her way.

I thought, as I drove down the new fast road to Southampton, dodged between the cars, overtook, braked suddenly, waited at a petrol station, 'England will seem small. When I get back, it will have shrunk. There will be too many people. All will be too close, too explicit.' I prepared myself for change; it was what I wanted. Too long a teacher, standing up before the dazzling stare of the class, too long a plump, dark person who painted, too long myself, twenty-seven years too long Ruby Smith, the same, predictable even to myself, the child, the girl, the woman; there must be something more. When I was five, I discovered what my name meant. My mother showed me a ruby ring, and told me. That was me, that glow under the blood, that winking fire closed in a velvet box; it did not matter that I had been called after my grandmother, who was fat and ordinary. And I never told Anna this, about my mother's ruby, for she had before her, each time she faced herself in the mirror, the explicit vision of her own excellence; but it made a difference. And as I drove, I thought on, 'This change I am looking for, this thing that will happen, it could only be a man; and yet how would a man find me out, when he has Anna before him?' The men who had paused to love me had never met Anna; I had, I realised now, not allowed them to; I felt my face grow hot, although I was alone. 'A French lover,' I mouthed to the driving mirror, making myself ridiculous, 'But what good will that be?' England would be the same when I came back, whatever the change in me; whether I returned dizzy with sex, transfigured by love, con-

15

verted to Catholicism or simply older, carrying my duty-free drink back to another cold winter; it would be small, tracked across with well-worn lines, the snailpaths of human endeavour, the air would be buzzing with complaint, and each small parcel of land would belong to somebody. People I met would stare curiously in that way they did, and ask me exactly what I meant, and my hands rising empty into the air would explain nothing. I felt, when I came to the Southampton docks and drove my old Citroën to the very edge, that I had been driven to this extremity of land, pushed by crowds of millions, edged to the corner, nudged towards the sea, and that before me, over such a narrow strip of water, the land was continuous and solid and unknown, all the way from Cherbourg and spreading through France, through central Europe, all the way out to the icy points where there is emptiness and clarity and the air crackling between countless trees, all the way to coasts where the sun turns stones to wax and all vegetation shrinks and dies, close to the matchblack earth. It is not so, I know. But space draws us like lemmings to the edge of our little patch, we need the illusion; and we plunge willingly over, simply in our longing for the unknown place.

Anna said to me once, when we were students, talking late at her parents' house, over cups of coffee, 'Which do you think is the most important, sex or friendship?' It was the age of absolutes, when in our ignorance we looked forward confidently to knowledge. I thought for the proper amount of time and answered, to the expectant silence between us, 'I

16

should think probably friendship.'

'Why?' she asked me, curious, respectful of my conclusion.

'Well, I suppose because sex doesn't last, and friendship does. Think of being old, one would need one's friends so much.' I knew, even as I said it, that this was weak; but how else at this moment when all seemed possible, could one decide?

'But we aren't old now,' she said, 'I was thinking of now. It's the present that matters, surely.'

'Well, yes, in a way.' I was confused, wanting to say that both were my due.

'I was going to say sex,' she continued, 'at least, I think it ought to be. It's the only way you can really get to know somebody, isn't it? The only way there can be no pretence?' She stared hard at me, a small frown gathered between her eyes, as though she were worried.

'I don't know,' I said, 'I should have thought there could be pretence. But, well, I think both are important. It just depends what you're looking for, don't you think?'

And she said, 'I don't know. But I shall know, I'm sure I shall. I somehow feel I shan't really have lived unless *that* happens – that sort of sex that lets you know, that makes you absolutely sure there hasn't been any cheating.'

I was impressed, I remember; we were both silent, musing on possibilities, both of us at the time virgins. Her look of rapt, searching concentration stayed with me that evening. She seemed to demand a meaning of life which I had not dared to imagine. At last I said, a little tentatively, 'But can't one be sure in friendship?'

And she replied, sighing, older I felt than I, 'But it isn't really enough, is it? There's got to be something more certain. There's got to be something more to look for.' In another age, she could have been a nun. I thought, as I began my journey, that I travelled still in her footsteps, that the paths marked out for me were still the ones she had chosen; and so she flew south, still dissatisfied, still searching, the young men who had loved her left behind, and so I followed, finding that my own life, its unhappy recent love and its fruitlessness, was fanned into restlessness by the vibration of her wings. 'Let's face it,' she had said, on that last occasion when we had met, 'They're none of them worth it. I ask you, what a lot of lame ducks we'd landed ourselves with. Poor old Ian, polishing his car up on Sunday mornings, think of him doing it still. And as for your rotten old John having the bad taste to marry a bird from Clapham. We can do better than this, darling, just you wait and see.' And on another occasion, when I had told her of my affair with the man who made violins in a shop in Bond Street, my inevitably prosaic John for all his purple corduroy, she had exclaimed, 'But it's not love, Ruby? It's not the real thing, is it? D'you mean to say you're actually in love?' and I, loosened from my composure, doubting my indistinct feelings, laughed and mocked with her and assured her that I, no more than she, had found the philosophers' stone.

And so I come to twilight in Cherbourg, to cafés lit and frequented by men in blue, cars pouring into the city and out on to the lonelier roads, carrying searchers in all directions to find their separate ends; to

18

darkness falling over Normandy, the apple-trees, the tall, wet orchards and the hidden houses, walled against the invader, the concrete littered beaches where sand blew long ago over lost footprints, the rooms where families sit over dinner and a long arm reaches for the wine; night settles over the peninsula, sea mist rises and enfolds its outlying points; inland the air is sharp and cool, apple-sharp, dewy, and the trees' points disappear into darkness along the roads; a car's lights sweep up yellow, and light the under-growth and are seen far away. There is a car travelling south, and I am in it, tired at the wheel, pushing on to find the first point on my journey, a certain village, a certain house, a certain bed for the night. The day's heat has passed, leaving warm only the red sides of houses, the walls where cats sit half-asleep. It is August, but already autumn breathes on the country nights, as if this were the true season. A rabbit dashes into the road – or is it a small cat? The eyes are red as it stares, then it rushes fumbling to the hedgerow and has gone. There are stars coming, pricking through darkness where the road climbs to meet the horizon; the sky lying close to the earth is still faintly red. The car draws into a lay-by, I pull the map out of the glove pocket, study it in a feeble light. It is a new map, not yet worn and crumpled with day-to-day checking and wondering and following its lines; no grimy fingers have traced ways upon it yet, nobody has bundled it hastily away without folding it, nobody has spilt coffee on it, or wine. It shows the road, twenty kilometres farther to the south, through the next town and then a turning to the left, a village hidden from the main road among trees and farms. It is folded and put away and the car starts again, with a sound that startles, and I see myself driving again, eyes strained, feet achingly poised, piercing the darkness that lies between each lighted tree as I pass it. The trees go with a sound like sleep broken, the kilometres slip by unmarked. Soon there will be an arrival. Brakes upon gravel, doors opening, a greeting, recognition; lighted rooms, food upon a table, familiar voices talking English in a foreign room. Coming suddenly into brilliance, it is hard to see; one blinks, stumbling back a little, wondering if this is right, as one's legs move stiffly and one's voice, unused over the hours to speech, grates upon the ear, the voice of a croaking stranger. With luck, there is reassurance and solicitude. The familiar certainties move back into their focus, and objects loom out of the vacuum, ordinary things; and yet still one sits, a little dazed, a little shocked, and longs for the smooth balancing of sleep. My first stage, at least, was accomplished.

I said after a bit, 'That friend I wrote to you about. Did she come? I thought it would be nice for her, on her way south.' We sat around a dark wooden square of table, a great bowl of soup at its centre, billowing steam when the lid was lifted. I smelled onions, leeks and potatoes and crumbled my bread in anticipation and dropped small pieces into my mouth. Howard poured wine, Jeannie carried the lid of the soup bowl away and came back flushed and brisk to sit down at the table.

'Soup, darling?'

'No thanks,' she said. 'I had so much supper. I'll

20

just have a cigarette, if you don't mind. And some more wine.' It was late and they had made soup for me and opened two litre bottles of wine; I sank back into the cushioned calm of their welcome; they had been expecting me and I had arrived.

'No, she didn't, actually,' Howard said, his New England voice clearer still, the way his hair grew so American; and yet they had settled here, far from home, and had somehow, as a couple, filled out. I wanted to ask him, as we stood at the door and looked out into darkness, as we moved leisurely around the kitchen, clearing up, about his life here and his work. But I had started talking about Anna, thrown in a little dart that set them arguing, in the measured routine way that married couples do.

'Well, she just might have,' Jeannie was saying, 'Only we might have been away. We went to Paris that week, didn't we? And she might just possibly have come while we were away. I forget when she was due to come. A week ago last Tuesday? The sixth, didn't you say?'

'No, honey, it wasn't that week we were away, we were back by the Tuesday, that was the day we had that picnic, remember? We left Paris on the Monday, I remember distinctly.'

'Howie, it was a Friday we came back. Don't you remember, I had to get that cut of meat ordered because those people were coming on the Saturday?' Her voice flattened out, became more emphatically mid-western, she leaned forward with her persistence drawing her face to a fine pointing muzzle. I saw her again as she had been, a crop-haired tomboy in bermudas and kneesocks, seeing Europe for the first

21

time. Now she was insistent, but at last her gaze dropped before Howard's, her long hair hid her angry cheeks, and she looked away.

'Anyway,' he said, 'what's it matter? Ruby doesn't want to know what day we were or weren't in Paris. She wants to know if we saw her friend. I'm sorry, Ruby, we didn't. Maybe we should have stayed, maybe it was rude of us to take off like that when you said she was coming; but I had to see my publisher, and Jeannie had a date with her dentist, she actually goes to Paris to get her teeth fixed, so, well, we just went. Still there's a hell of a lot of France to see. I just hope she found a welcome some place else. Why'n't you both come and spend a few days on your way back, anyway?'

'Hey, wait a minute, she'd have arrived when Caley was here, wouldn't she?' Jeannie was alert with her ideas, her flush receding because she had found the answer.

I began to say, 'Well, it really doesn't matter,' but my murmur died before their enthusiasm. I wondered how they were not yet burnt up by their fierce concentration upon the details of life; and I was tired still, I flagged before their vigour and could only listen.

'Why, yes, so she would. Yeah, if that was the week we were away. Okay, Jeannie, so that was the week we were away, you win, let's call it quits. Yeah, we had this friend of mine staying here, and he wasn't due to leave till the day we came back, we had a lot to talk about, but I guess he must have had another engagement, or maybe the wine ran out, because he'd blown by the time we got back.'

22

'It must've been the wine,' Jeannie said, 'There wasn't a drop left in the cellar when we got home. I can't imagine how he got through all that on his own.'

'Then you don't know Caley like I do,' her husband said, his gentle smile moving from her to me, to show me he loved and teased her, and found her innocent.

'Unless of course Ruby's friend helped him,' Jeannie said, 'If she came.'

I yawned and shivered, and found my hands shaking, as if in a state of shock, as if the vibrations of travelling still moved me. I felt them far from me and watched them move as a slow fish at the pond's bottom might watch the quick flickerings of water spiders against the remote light of day. 'Who's Caley?' I asked them, wanting with some part of me at least to discover.

'Friend of Howie's,' Jeannie said, 'College friend, wasn't he; lived in New York for a while when we did, now travelling Europe, another expatriate, looking for a change of scene. God knows where he's got to now, but I guess he'll be back for the long winter evenings.'

'I don't suppose Anna came,' I said. I did not suppose, really, that she would have stayed. I saw her glance tentatively round the door, her arched English lady eyebrows, her hair swinging forward, saw the drunken American, like a cowboy, boots upon the mantelpiece probably and bottles at his side, guns or packs of cards somewhere, and a leer from under hairy eyebrows. 'I think your drunken friend might have scared her off, if she did.'

'God, what do you read, Buffalo Bill comics?'

'Caley's an intellectual, too,' Jeannie said, like a

mother protecting a young son, 'Caley writes as well.'

'Caley's not an intellectual, he's a roughneck poet,' Howard said, 'Caley just brings it all up from his guts. He hasn't got an intellect, Caley, he's just got dreams in the top storey and sex down below, and poetry spewing out from halfway between the two, if you ask me. But he's hardly enough to frighten a nice young English girl away.'

I said, 'Oh, she's not that young. She's the same age as me.'

'Okay, a nice middle-aged English spinster, then.' He smiled, telling me it was not true, as if I myself had not asked him to salt the wound. 'Has he been published, your friend?' I asked, but neither of them seemed to know. I looked about the room for signs of Anna, wanting a tipped English cigarette, a handkerchief, a small testimony to her presence. It would be good to know whether she had been here or not. I do not like things to be left unfinished, but seek a clear picture of what has been, so that I may imagine what is yet to come. And somewhere the old suspicion of adolescence raised its head, the beginning of the fear that I had been excluded. I would never see Anna peering round that door, greeting with her ladylike astonishment the roughneck poet. That picture was gone.

It was early morning when we went to bed, and I in my tiredness, my lassitude, had allowed them to pull me close again, to recreate me as my self of six years ago, so that the present, London, my job, all fell away. Time slipped away, our talk was blurred by wine, their presence was no longer alien but familiar, I loved them with a shock of pleasure all over again;

24

for it had been before, this friendship, when Howard was over in Cambridge on a research grant, Jeannie a tourist falling in love, and I, a dabbler, a painter, a girl growing into her twenties with neither face nor fortune but a clown's eagerness to please. It seemed strange now that neither of them had met Anna; in a way, it made them more specifically mine, it made my closeness to them safe, and now they had missed her again, so that the circle was still intact.

'No great love in your life, then?' Jeannie spoke lightly, but wanted intensely to know why I had not married. I saw the sucking-in of a corner of Howard's mouth, as if he waited with anxiety, disapproving.

'Not really,' I said carelessly, letting them off. 'Just a few small ones. No Mister Right, at any rate, so you can go on hatching plots for me.' And they laughed and began to talk of something else. I envied them their decisions, their ability to move together; to get married, to live in France, to have one's own vegetables growing in the plot of land outside, this was achievement. Their travelling was over, for the moment at least, and this place that they had found drew me to its centre like a closing sea anemone, inviting me to stay. I wanted to stay and settle and be included, to be a child safe between two adults, making myself safely at home. And yet this was to be only the first place on my journey and there was no point in unpacking my suitcase, even in getting everything out of the car; certainly no point in unpacking all my mind. The traveller must will himself to reserve, to hold something back, or otherwise there is no journey; he wants to be a child and enfolded, and instead he must be the perpetual adolescent, thrown out again and again from the hearth, the home, set upon another road to another place, firmly put out of doors to find his own way. To relax before another's fire and spread all one's treasures around is to risk the cold awakening, the voice at dawn that summons with the call to go. There must be stages on the way, but no arrivals. Talking to Howard and Jeannie, envying them their warm, bickering, lively hold upon each other, sleeping alone in their spare bed with the debris of wine bottles and cigarettes around me, I was tired already, and dissatisfied, with what I had undertaken. There was only wayward Anna, somewhere on ahead of me, to make me go on; and the will to follow was not mine.

That night I was too tired and dazed to wash, too feeble to do anything but get thankfully into the bed they had prepared for me. I sat against the pillows in my nightdress, and Howard stood over me like a father and asked with his grave politeness if I had all I needed. The sheets were rough and clean, having hung to dry in the sun, the duvet plump as a meringue over me. Physical comfort, the relief of the nearness of sleep, had at last pushed all thought away.

'Fine, thanks. You are good. It is lovely. All of it's lovely.' And I slept. But in the morning I was in the bathroom before either of them, when Jeannie was in the kitchen in her dressing-gown, making coffee, and Howard in bed still, reading the paper. I unpacked my new things from my sponge-bag – toothbrush, flannel, toothpaste, soap – as for going back to school, one buys these things new for a journey; the illusion is of having turned a new leaf, of beginning again. I had dropped all my old ones into the dustbin.

26

But as I rinsed the toothpaste from my mouth, I
noticed in a corner of the bathroom an empty,
squashed tube of English toothpaste that had been
tortured and trodden on to get the last squeeze out,
and thrown angrily away, to miss the waste-paper
basket. I looked about; Howard's and Jeannie's tooth-
brushes stood side by side in a glass, and beside them
was some special Swiss toothpaste made of salt. I
picked up the twisted tube of Maclean's and put it in
my dressing-gown pocket. A question I had hardly
asked had been answered. One did not take out one's
toothpaste unless one intended to stay, at least for a
night.

At last my friends were waving me away, turning
back into their house to continue their lives; waiting
until I was nearly at the turn of the road, turning
away just before I reached the corner, their waving
over before I was truly gone. I saw their backs for a
second in the mirror, a tall man and a short woman,
turning back towards their house. They could, in that
instant, have been anybody, any couple with a house
to live in, who will take in visitors as a matter of
course, and include them, and let them go; because
the reality of life is between the two of them, unin-
terrupted. But now, before me, the morning was
misty with the promise of heat, thickly pale blue,
sunshine beginning on the leaves. The road was
fairly empty, for it was still early; I had far to go,
and the actual way, the uncurling morning, took my
attention from what I could never know, to what was
before me. I sang, and the mist lifted, and it was
after all easy to leave and take my way, the hands
that had received me having tipped me lightly, a

pigeon from a basket, into the morning air, the day
new, whole to itself, separated from stale yesterday
as if a table had been wiped clean. There are days
which seem to have been washed, early in the morning, which start with such hope that by midday they
can only be a blazing miracle, by evening they have
changed and mellowed and set one at rest; it was a
day like that, or I think I should have looked a little
longer backward. As it was, my eyes followed my
pointing car bonnet towards the south, and I rolled
the windows down and filled my eyes and lungs with
the beauty of rural France, and thought, I shall stop
when I am hungry or when I am tired, for by some
incredible grace I am free. Nobody depends upon
me, nobody makes patterns of my life; the old
dilemmas of existence are truly left behind.

John had asked me, 'Why France, particularly?' at
that last conversation of ours, months ago, that was
more like an interview.

'Why France? Because I know it, I suppose. Home
only not-home, you know.'

'I don't see the point,' he said then, 'of travelling,
unless you go somewhere you've never been before.
I'd fly somewhere really exciting, if I were you.' And
I thought, but did not say to him – for he had made
himself overnight a stranger – I cannot take anything
now that is too strange, too unknown; I must have a
few landmarks on my journey.

I said, 'Everybody travels for different reasons'; and
he was silent, thinking, I suppose, that I travelled to
make myself forget. He was guilty, solicitous, longing
to have me go. I asked him, 'Where are you going for
your honeymoon, then?' and he answered, 'Portugal'

and I left him quickly after that, for to see a person so embarrassed when love for him has not entirely gone is a painful humiliation.

To Anna I said, 'It's all over,' and assumed for the first time a lightness of tone, an irony, with which I would for ever after mention him; I assumed the wound healed, and she, with her friendliness and cynicism, assured me that it was he, not I, who had been tried and found wanting.

'France'll be the thing,' she told me. 'Just think of it. And what's one man, anyway, in a world of millions? There are lots where he came from, Rube, and you deserve the very best.' But it was too quick, I felt, too glib; and was it that Anna in her triumphant gaiety could not admit the presence of suffering, or did she care for my feelings so that she had to see me whole again? I had always given her, since the earliest years, the benefit of the doubt that she accorded me, I had always trusted her integrity. And now, miraculously free, as she had promised, of my troubles, I trusted her to be right, to find whatever would prove to be my salvation; deeper into France I followed her, taking the same road.

The land exists, independent of the travellers who pass and invest it with their dreams. Poplars blowing in the slight wind, green fields untracked by feet of cattle or of men, landscapes created in light by spots that have dropped from a brush, the blond cows passing slowly down a lane. It is not long before the Loire appears like a slow grey-green sea, the first great river of France moving in its separate swirls and eddies between the dust-grey bushy trees upon its banks. So far apart, these banks; a bridge spans the great gap as if it can only just, stretching and stretching, reach to the other side. The city sprawls around the river, cafés on terraces placed to turn all faces down to the inscrutable flood, smaller bridges like arms, pulling the earth together, cars moving in a slow gleam from bank to bank. In places the water has drawn back to leave patches of mud shining; there are shallow falls where men stand fishing in their narrow boats, beaches of dulled sand, cordoned off, where children play. In the city, heat is intense, thudding upon earth, shrieking upon metal. Policemen stand and the traffic revolves, cars and *camions* crowding upon each other at the rise of a hand, released again by the flamboyant sweep to move them on. The land is divided, and men play upon it, juggling upon the river banks. Up through the city, on the other side, the road moves on past a great crouching castle in its trees, and away among the vineyards. There are vines everywhere now, young green leaves and the grapes still small, the shallow hills used and used again. The road leaves the city and further on there is a village, where one might stop to taste wine under canopies of leaves, or buy a sandwich, or drink Pernod and water at a roadside café, fine dust around the feet, the hot sour breath of the lorries in one's nose. One might stop here and buy a postcard and sit for a moment in the shade, wondering what to write, decide upon something inconclusive, banal, stick on a stamp licked with a tongue already dry again and scrawl words in a hurry, because all are inadequate, and post it, simply because one passed in the sleeping square a slit in the wall for letters. One might equally

30

stop alone, or in the company of another; there are couples strolling here already, and solitary men smoking in the shade, and families with children, hot and grumbling. One might sit, watching a gypsy girl cross the square to sell baskets and beg in a flat, sad tone for money; one might even buy a basket and see that sullen face flicker alive before it abruptly turns away. Anybody might stop here, simply because the road is long, the view to the far river a vision of temporary peace; and again, drawn southwards to the way that is called la Route du Vin, pestered by the vision of a bacchic idyll waiting always farther on, anybody might leap to his feet and decide in an instant with his companion to take the road again and join the hunt questing after the perfection promised in a word. Shadows fall sharply here, cleaving the light; the square is patterned under the bright leaves of the plane-tree in its basket; yet behind the very clarity of light and shade a thousand images move and flicker, a shadow detaches itself and becomes a nun walking, geranium leaves under a café awning shudder and become a man drinking anis, the obscurity under a tin table releases a dog, who crawls out and shakes himself in the sun. On a chequered table top, the shadows of branches part for a moment and the small twigs are the veins in a man's hand, that is closed tightly upon a woman's, as a decision is made. The eye turns bewildered from shade to brilliance, dances with red patternings, finds the marks of hooves and chains imprinted on the sky. One might take dark glasses from a handbag and fit them upon a slippery nose and move away in time with another, all eyes following, across the square, back to the safety of a moving car and the purpose of the road.

'I ought to let my friend know.'
'Know what?'
'Well – I'm supposed to be meeting her in a week.'
'There's still the week.'
'Damn, I wish to God I hadn't arranged it.'
'We can fix something, can't we? She's old enough to be out on her own?'
'I suppose. But she's so – at the moment, anyway – so vulnerable. I don't really want to let her down. She's had a busted love affair, you know. I feel sort of responsible for her, in a way.'
'Well, as I say, we've got a week. We can find her and tell her, if you like. We needn't rat on her. And anything can happen in a week, hell.'
'I suppose it can.'

I was not, I realised as I crossed the Loire, going to be anywhere near the Lot valley that night. The painting school and Anna were going to have to wait a day for me; I was going to spend the night in an hotel, eat dinner at the solitary table – one flower, a tiny carafe of wine – set for a woman dining alone; I would breakfast alone, among the munching men reading local farming papers, and travel on tomorrow, down through the Dordogne, to my destination. Before leaving, I had hardly looked at my map; and now France stretched all around me, as well as on that folded square of paper, larger than I had remembered, emptier than I had dreamed. Between each town there were whole stories and tapestries, and at

32

the feet of industry and farming, the flowered animal paradise of Les Très Riches Heures and the hunting scenes I loved. To go too fast was appalling; and even now, turning my eyes from the invitation of the countryside sternly back to the road again, I was going too fast. Each lighted window, each face in the street persuaded me continually to stop; but it was soon evening again, and I was on the edge of the Dordogne forests, where the pigs I am told hunt like addicts in the dark; I had travelled, time had moved; nothing, not even the texture of the grass, remained the same.

Anna, I remembered, would have travelled this same road, leaving the Sandersons' house perhaps as I had done, early in the morning and full of hope. She too would have stopped upon the road, entered an hotel gingerly, with the apology of women alone, to ask if there were a room for the night. She too would have studied the menu as I now studied it, and eaten its courses rather too quickly, because there was no-body opposite to lean gently over in conversation, and pour the wine during a scarcely perceptible gap in the flow of laughter and words; like me, she would perhaps have felt all at once too full, as if there were something disgusting about it all. She would have done this, I thought, as I crossed the bar to go up-stairs after my dinner, drawing men's glances after me and shrugging them off with my briskness, but she would have done it in her own unshakeable way. Anna eating dinner alone in a restaurant would be a tragic figure, a woman to whom fate had been unkind. I was simply myself, trying ungracefully to manage my life alone. We have, though, the same lack, the same insufficiency; in France, above all places, the figure opposite must be a man. Food, spread out lovingly over several courses, cooked separately and with care, becomes no longer simply food, but a ritual offering; and its end, perhaps, after the tasting and drinking and the mood growing and spreading, the click of the last knife upon the plate, can only be a willing seduction of some kind. And so I forgot to taste my soup, my golden fish and the beef stew in wine that followed, and I went to bed early and drew the shutters tight, and in the morning, with a sense of failure, drank up my coffee quickly and ate only one piece of bread and jam, and smoked a cigarette on my way to the car, for fear of lingering. The sense of my own freedom and self-sufficiency which had come to me unexpectedly as I left the Sandersons yesterday morning had grown thinner and become transparent after hours of solitude, and now, like a waning moon, had nearly disappeared. I angrily choked the car with petrol, trying to make it start; the rattle of the engine trying to turn over echoed in the empty garage. I had to wait a painful minute. Forcing myself to be gentle, I tried again, one foot lightly upon the accelerator, my hands nervous around the wheel. There was nobody to see me back out of the garage and turn into the little yard, nobody to wave and wish me a good journey; and it is upon these things that the freedom to go depends; if nobody noticed one's arrival, one's departure can have little significance; the traveller, I found, who has no destination has only the ghostly freedom of the Flying Dutchman, the freedom to go always on, which is rather a condemnation, the self-

34

sufficiency grown to shield him from the blankness in men's eyes. I wanted only now to arrive, to meet Anna, to find a welcome at the painting school and to be the self that others saw and expected. After just one short day and night alone upon the road, I wanted to see the faces in the drive, faces not questioning, not surprised, but expecting me. Anna's face, her ribaldry, her mocking 'So, you've got here at last?' her amusing stories about all that had caught her eye; a friend in a foreign land; a confirmation.

'So, you got here at last?'

Of course I am expected. I am easy, nonchalant in my reply, discounting the occasional doubts of the journey. 'Yes, I had got here. Good journey on the whole. How was yours?'

'Oh, fine, fine. Lovely weather, too.' With such easy platitudes, one rediscovers an old situation. Friends are friends, wherever. We are together again on a joint venture, the whole of France lies tamed at our feet. We have regained, in meeting each other as expected, our defences against the unruly world. Together, it seems that we know who we individually are. So the talk, the unwinding, the stories, the comparisons run in my head as I drive, the words are real enough, I hear them echo in the room where we will meet. My fantasy of safety exists; and who can say that it is not part of the whole? 'You got here at last.' I wait to hear it, and in my expectation ignore the reality I find.

The house stands high upon a hill, with meadows sloping away from it and a rough track winding up between them, banked with small trees and wild rose

35

bushes and tall yellow grass. One goes first to the village and asks in the shop or the café for the Fairbrothers, the English people, the English household, painters. But before the words are out, everybody has noticed the English car number plates, and there is no doubt where one is bound. It has been running for five years or so, every summer, this English painting school, and hundreds of people in hundreds of cars have during this time drawn up in the little square before the church of Saint-Louis, and turned their Michelin maps round anxiously in their hands, puzzling to find the right road, and under the eyes of the locals who know already, have entered the little shop and peered through the darkness to ask for cigarettes, chocolate, stumble into French and wave their arms oddly to indicate painting. Hundreds of times the little boys have run up, insistently calling, 'C'est là-bas, monsieur, madame – sur la colline là-bas, vous voyez!' and again and again the English cars have turned laboriously, churning the dust, to follow the narrow road which becomes a track, which opens into the forecourt of the house. How could the woman in the shop ever remember the faces even of recent comers or distinguish between features that searched for her anxiously through the shuttered gloom of her shop? How would even the sharpest-eyed boy recollect a certain number plate, a certain make of car? And how would the ageing man cutting away undergrowth on the hillside with a curved blade, straightening momentarily to watch another visitor grind on upwards in a cloud of white, ever focus on the close and moving car, seen for a moment, when his eyes are habitually stretched to watch

36

the horizon and check the massing clouds for hints of rain? So many must have come and gone.

There were no faces in the drive as I ground up in first gear, braked and opened the door to stretch my legs. There were only cars, parked in an orderly way along the wall of the house, cars covered with white dust, with English number plates. The large clear letters on the plates looked odd, the cars themselves, with sketch pads and bottles of insect repellent and paper handkerchiefs lying against the rear windows, looked odd. But the house looked right, as if it had grown there, a long, comfortable courtyard house with the secretive look of French houses on hot days when the shutters are closed. The roof tiles rippled and were bleached pink like cloth; under the eaves were deep black slits, the eyes of the attic where tobacco was stored. A cat in the driveway looked at me, yawned and looked away. There was a white handkerchief, lying in a white trapezium as if it had been drawn out like that by the wind, when somebody had waved it. I walked towards the house, stumbling a little on the sharp white stones in my sandals, past the blind façade of the house in its siesta and round through the courtyard to approach an open door. I heard voices, and someone came running across the courtyard behind me, a girl wearing a dress that looked Greek, her long dark hair floating about on her shoulders, her bare white arms and legs fragile, even rickety.

'Hallo,' she gasped, and I wondered why she had run.

'Hallo. I've come to . . .'

'Oh, you've come to see Thomas and Kirstin. Well,

Thomas is taking a class at the moment – look, there they are.' I glanced where she pointed, and saw higher on the hill the white blobs of drawings just begun, the coloured blobs of people bending over them. 'But Kirstin's inside,' she went on breathlessly, 'so I'm sure it'd be all right if you came in. I'm her daughter, actually. My name's Tamsin.'

'I'm Ruby Smith,' I said, 'and I've come to join the course. I don't suppose you can tell me . . .'

'Oh, yes,' she said, 'I'm sure they can fit you in.'

'I booked, though, I mean, I wrote. They're expecting me.'

'Well, of course,' she smiled, a faded Botticelli, 'I'm sure that's all right, only you see, they have so many people. We've got forty-eight staying at the moment, and we have all our meals out here in the barn, and the most wonderful discussions, oh, and dancing and everything. Do come in. I'll just see if Kirstin can see you.'

She knocked on an inside door, leaning close to it, tapping with one knuckle, her face drawn with reverence. I stood beside her and looked at a row of about thirty hats, hanging from hooks, whose owners had perhaps hung them casually there, and then entered the house, and never returned.

'Yes, do go in,' Tamsin whispered. 'She's been resting, but she can see you now.'

'Darling, coffee,' sounded a voice from within, 'coffee for two, will you, oh and two brandies. Yes, do come in.'

I entered a long room and felt at once as if I stood on the deck of a ship, for all the long windows were open on this side of the house, and below, the valley

38

waved and curled, a solid sea. Sun and maize fields like golden water, and the sky blue coming right into the room, for the walls between the beams, and the ceiling were painted blue, and there were tall, blue glasses and a blue crazed bowl, and blue flowers sprouting near the hearth. But the clearest, hardest blue drew my gaze at last, the eyes of the woman seated in a long wicker chair beside the window, smoking a cigarette. She stared at me, her eyes like chips of china, and said, 'Do sit down. Do tell me your name. I'm Kirstin. You will have coffee, won't you. Oh, and you will have a brandy. Cigarette? I've ordered two brandies, anyway. Now, do tell me, where are you from?'

'I'm Ruby Smith,' I said, 'I wrote, I mean we wrote, my friend Anna Parrish, I believe you know her, a friend of a friend, I believe. Somebody called Judith Reeves?'

'Oh, Judith,' she smiled, 'Oh, yes. Now do tell me, how do you know Judith? Have you been to her cottage in Wales? Oh, we used to have a marvellous time there before the war.'

'I don't actually know her,' I said, 'But this friend of mine, Anna Parrish, got your address from her, and we wrote to you, if you remember, and Anna is here now. I've come on to join her, you see.' I spoke a little aggressively; I saw an easy defence rise in those piercing eyes.

'Now, I don't quite understand,' she said. 'You say she is here now?'

'Yes,' I said, staring back at her, determined now, 'she came last week, and I was due here yesterday, but I had to spend the night in a hotel on the way.

My name is Ruby Smith, and I teach art. She's called
Anna Parrish, and she's a painter, she's got straight
blond hair which she sometimes wears loose, sometimes in a kind of bun. She's taller than me, about
five foot eight, she has a Mini with an estate back,
she wears sort of trouser suits, frilly blouses, rather
smart. You must know who I mean. She must be
here.'

'Oh,' Kirstin Fairbrother said, 'Oh, yes. Oh, I think
I know who you mean. Rather beautiful person,
doesn't talk all that much. A bit ice-maiden looking.'

'Yes, yes, that sounds like Anna. She is here, then?'

The door opened slowly, as if whoever was opening it had her hands full. Tamsin, with the tray of
coffee and brandy came across the room and set the
tray unsteadily on a little table. Another girl, younger,
with the same pale features, followed her and crossed
to the cupboard in the corner, brought out two of the
veined blue glasses and set them down. With a nervous movement, Tamsin pushed back her hair, blink-
ing at her mother as if uncertain what to do next,
standing there with her shoulders bent.

'Thanks,' Kirstin said, not looking at her. 'Oh,
you've met my daughter I suppose? This is Tamsin.
The other one's Rose, she's not mine.' I expected
them almost to go out backwards, bowing; but they
turned and walked away with their strange creeping
step, reminding me of nuns.

'Now, coffee, sugar? Where were we? Oh, yes,
your friend. Well, unless I'm mistaken, she had
trouble with her car on the way here, gasket went
or something, I don't really know about these things.
So she got a lift here, left the car in a garage some-

where. Yes, I think she went back to fetch it, and she was going to be back by tomorrow, because tomorrow, that's it, Thomas is taking them all on an expedition somewhere, and she didn't want to miss it. And then in the evening we dance. Do you dance? I was a ballet dancer, you see. I simply have to go on dancing. Oh, you'll enjoy that.' She stood up, as if to demonstrate something; a tall, well-proportioned woman, moving gracefully, her hair bleached and coiled elaborately, her legs beneath her short, flared skirt coming out at the calf with the curve of a dancer's, shapely, unveined. From the back, she could have been forty, even thirty-five; it was only that face, lined and pale and decorated clownishly with make-up, that gave her away; she must have been at least fifty. But the eyes, I imagined, had not changed. They were the eyes of decision, of ruthlessness. She had got what she wanted. And I realised, as she began to speak to me again, that the strange thing about them was that they never appeared to blink; like a reptile's eyes, they were unmoving.

'How odd,' I said. 'I thought she had her car serviced before she came. Still, it's always on holiday that things like that happen, isn't it? Well,' I said jovially, pushing her, 'It's marvellous to have arrived. Now do tell me about the course.'

Time moved smoothly in this house, each section of the day set aside for particular people to do particular things. Under the disguise of spontaneity, each action had been planned. Meals appeared, carried with the same silent subservience I had noticed in Tamsin and Rose; there seemed to be a whole troop of young people engaged in adoration of the Fairbrothers, girls with the sleek bent heads of madonnas and the eyes of acolytes, boys in ragged jeans and dyed vests, smoking endless cigarettes and following Thomas with their gaze. They were in turn the chorus, the procession, the household slaves.

'Don't you think Kirstin's fabulous?' one of them said to me as I helped to dry the wine glasses and put them away. 'She's so sort of vital. She doesn't seem like one of that generation, d'you think?' This was Margot, tough and sunburnt in her bell-bottomed trousers, pink shirt knotted under her breasts to leave her midriff bare. I was surprised; she looked healthier, more ordinary than the others.

'Well,' I said, 'I suppose she is rather extra-ordinary.'

She looked at me, brows raised; my voice had hesitated. 'And Thomas,' she said; 'Of course, he's the most marvellous painter. But somehow, the thing for me here is the atmosphere. You know? There are so few places in the world that are really congenial. And they're such a marvellous couple. So comple-mentary. Almost enough to make one think marriage isn't such a bad idea, after all.' She laughed at me, and I laughed easily, as if I agreed. We hung the sodden cloths on the window sill to dry and crossed the cool stone kitchen to the back door.

'You a painter?' I asked her, as conversation had dwindled away.

'Sort of. I used to go to art school, but found it all rather cramped. I can't stand England, actually, let alone Kingston-on-Thames. So phoney, the whole set-up. I can't really paint unless I'm feeling good.

You know, one needs a certain milieu.'

Her voice was caught in Kirstin's phrases like a fly in a web; I wanted to shake myself, to be free; the web stretched between the very walls of this place and hung bright in the air between the twos and threes who sat chatting on the steps, in the sun, spun about the eyes and ears until all was false. I had only been there a few hours, and I began to suspect the story about Anna's car. It seemed far more likely that she had made her escape, and would only return to find me and whisk me away. I saw her blank, polite face before Margot's enthusiasm, her sarcasm at the groups of acolytes, her hair fall across her eyes, hiding her true expression, as she listened to Kirstin. But there were the paintings, hung all around the walls, the proof in Thomas's light-filled canvases that underneath it all there was a spark, a reality; the stone we had all come, originally, to touch.

A young man joined us, as we settled in a patch of shade, together through inertia, to smoke our after-lunch cigarettes. He was slight, dark, immaculate. He offered round a large pack of Benson and Hedges and lit one for himself, unperturbed by our preferring to smoke Gauloises. There was half an hour yet before the afternoon session began, and little to say.

'Oh, everyone paints, don't they? I'm more an observer, I suppose.'

'Are you on the course?'

'No. no. Just visiting. I thought I'd drop in and have a look, see what sort of a scene it was.'

'What sort of a scene is it?'

'Well, not my sort of scene, as far as I can tell. I

mean, she'd eat you as soon as look at you, wouldn't she?'

'What on earth do you mean?' Margot stiffened; and at that moment Kirstin herself, languid from her afternoon sleep in a loosely tied kimono, came down the steps and joined us.

'Hallo, darlings. Anyone got a cigarette for me?' The young dark man shot out his packet again, so that it lay before her, gleaming. 'How kind. Now, how are you getting on? David, I must show you round before you go; it was David, wasn't it?'

He inclined his head, a dumb reverence stealing his former bravado.

'You know, it's extraordinary, really, but I'm quite sure I must have seen you before somewhere. I'm not a person who forgets facts. I think it must be living with a painter for so long, perhaps. It's so marvellously good for one. It makes one so receptive of new impressions, so visually alive. Tell me, do you know the Armstrongs?'

'Philip Armstrong? Well, I don't exactly know him, but of course I know his work. Marvellous – incredible feeling for texture, don't you think?' She had run her fingers over him, feeling for the essential switch; he would never again criticise the place, nor her, for he was converted. As if she searched with blind fingers through a heap of keys, feeling for the one that would fit the lock, she sifted and discarded several hundred approaches, and found the right one; the key fitted his vanity, his longing to associate with the successful.

'Well, I have the feeling that I must have met you at one of his parties. Of course, you know the parties

44

he gives. Such fun, although it's always a nuisance to get home from Putney. No, don't tell me, I'm sure you must have been there last Christmas; the time darling Christophe danced on the table? I'm positive I saw you there.'

And the dark young man said humbly, 'Yes, perhaps you did.'

'Come on, let me show you our estate,' she begged him, jumping up like a girl, throwing her half-smoked cigarette down and grinding it out with a sandal toe, her foot arched beautifully, like a dancer's. She pulled her floating garment around her, tightened the silk sash at the waist until the breasts above it jutted and trembled in the concealing folds. I saw his blush, his nervousness; she held out her arm to him, and he walked with her stiffly across the courtyard. Margot sighed. 'It's not fair, is is? But then, there are some women that men simply can't resist. They simply have some kind of aura.'

'What about Thomas?' I asked, curious enough to pursue the conversation.

'Thomas?' She gave me a strange look, her eyes narrowed against the sun as she drew on her cigarette. 'Oh, Thomas doesn't mind. After all, they're making pots out of this place, aren't they? They just both do what they like. It's frightfully civilised really, don't you think?'

'You mean,' I said, 'she lures people here, and he makes money out of them?' Anger had been rising in me all afternoon, making me want to shatter and destroy. Margot said, 'No, I don't mean that at all. I told you, people come because of the atmosphere. He's a real painter, too, you know.'

'Oh, yes,' I said, 'he is. But do people come to learn to paint, or what?'

She stubbed out her cigarette and scowled at me. 'Yes, of course they do. If you must see the worst in everything, that's what you'll see. There's more than one way of looking at things, after all.' And I had to admit that she was right. I waited, while Anna was away, to discover what would be the key that she, Kirstin, held to unlock me, to assuage the doubts, silence the criticism, enrol me by my own still un-disclosed weakness into this big, happy family of hers.

I did not have to wait long. Afternoon became evening, and I came back down the hill with a crowd of others, under my arm an embryonic drawing of the great chestnut trees, the valley beyond. I had not been trying; my trees looked like doughnuts dotted with sugar, my house a bellied animal slithering down the hill; my mind had been elsewhere, my hand a stiff and useless instrument doing another's will, without the courage to lie still and do nothing. The fall and rise of the rich French countryside, down to the river, had told me nothing except that I wanted to follow its path to the horizon, and leave. Dinner was waiting upon the long trestled tables in the barn, as I came downstairs after a wash and a change of clothes, a sparse meal between the many long loaves that had burst like great ears of corn in the oven and the bottles of wine that stood in ranks. Garlic sausage and olives, followed by enormous pots of rice with a few mushrooms and pieces of bacon hiding in them, and then fruit. I was weak with hun-ger and sat between the silent Tamsin and a boy

46

from Esher called Robert, and filled myself with rice and bread once the sausage had run out, tipping down glass after glassful of wine. Across the table sat David, whose plans for leaving had evidently been shelved; his eyes travelling up to where Kirstin sat beside Thomas, his cheeks burning with exhilaration, or perhaps shame. The troop was silent, concentrating on feeding. At the bottom of the table sat the very few older people who had come, burying their heads in their dishes like teenagers, as if to survive they must pretend to youth and hunger. A grey-haired man with a gentle face had sausage skins stuck between his teeth, and his fingers and jaw twitched as he tried to save himself, sucking at his teeth like a horse and incapable of speech, when he was asked clearly if he would like some more. At last the girls, one behind the other and moving as deliberately as cattle, had carried the last dishes away. Thomas alone was left seated, a half-empty wine bottle before him from which he was filling his glass. He leaned back, a king granted everything by his court. The boys were pushing back the other tables against the wall of the barn, as if they rose and did their bit at the slightest signal, imperceptible to outsiders. Thomas cut himself a slice from the small round cheese that had been set before him, that he ate instead of rice.

He was alone in the company, by his own wishes not observed; all eyes were towards Kirstin, to begin. She waved a hand and called out across the courtyard to somebody in the house, the light was on in the long living-room and a sudden shout of music reached us through the open windows: Tchaikovsky,

I realised, the 1812 overture, a strange choice in France in the year of Napoleon's centenary; but she took it as her tune, bombastic and warlike, her own invincibility to ring out finally with the bells. She spread a hand, balanced, and began to dance. David, who had been at her side, stood back but could not step away from her enough to mix again with the crowd who stood to watch. Her back arched, she shook her head and lifted her feet in the precision of ballet while her body shook with a belly-dancer's wildness. It was a strange hybrid movement, growing so that the two elements blended, while she herself, moving faster, achieved a splendour that was neither of the ballet school nor the brothel, something that was her own and therefore pure, expressed in the proud concentration of her features that were closed against her audience. I had to admire her, for in those few minutes all falseness had fallen away; I saw her dancing for herself as I had never thought she would, being herself in a way that demanded neither praise nor censure. The envy in me was for the proportion and vigour of her body, she who was twenty-five years older than I, and for the inspiration to dance there and then; but most of all for the knowledge she had, under all that affectation, of who she was. This is me, she was saying with each movement; I have known the long hours of the ballet school and the brief triumphs of the strange bed; I am both expert and amateur, penitent and whore; but this, anyway, is me. And I, who did not know what was in me, found myself drawn to the forefront, watching her as if each movement of hers must draw some echo from my untrained and clumsy body, that knew only how

48

to react. So this is it, some small portion of my mind was saying, this is the magic, why they are all here. Those girls with their meek heads and the shuffle of servants, the gleam of admiration in their eyes, had come for this, whether they knew it or not: to watch another's self-realisation and in their passivity, their emulation, forego their own. And the young men, who trooped off after Thomas to learn to look at landscape and find the possibilities of paint; they too found their eyes drawn away from their canvases, their minds taken from their single path; as they watched Kirstin dance, and took her arm to cross the courtyard, and received her caress at the garden wall, as she took them to her room and gave them licence, they thought she would make men of them, they expected a certainty; and they stayed and stayed, because all they received was doubt. For she was fixed, she knew her extensions and her limits; they were all in the dance. No young lover was going to change her, and that essential part of making love in which the lover demands to see his partners changed beneath him would always be denied. Nothing was going to change Kirstin, for she knew it all already, she was fixed. A man looking into her eyes would see only the opaque reiteration of herself, no mirror of his own generosity. He would never know, and never dare to ask, if he had failed.

So this, I thought, is how it works; and as now the dance had changed, and she was trying to include David and make him twirl about her, like a cape, like a sword, and he became her accessory, I felt my anger grow again, my wonder suspended. At that moment it became clear that I must leave, if I was not to become an accessory against my will, a victim living out my life vicariously in her shade. Tomorrow, I said, as soon as Anna comes back, I will leave. Even if Anna wants to stay, I shall go.

A car was climbing the steep road from the valley, seen from afar on all sides as morning sun caught the gleam of glass and the duller coloured metal. As it left the main road and bumped up over the rough track, dust rose about it in clouds, obscuring it; one could only see the moving billow of white against ashen foliage. It turned into the driveway of the house and stopped behind the other cars, and for a moment all was still. Then the door opened and a figure got out, one solitary person, and stood for a moment beside the car, locking its door. The sun lit a fair head, white hands moving. The rest of the figure was green, from head to toes, with a flutter of white at the neck. Something black swung from the shoulder, a bag perhaps, or a brace of dead black birds. I put on my glasses and leaned upon the sill, my pencils and brushes already there beside me for the morning's class. The figure, moving towards the house with a feminine swing of the hips in a grass-green trouser suit, her eyes invisible behind great round dark glasses, came towards me slowly, as if unhurried, yet never paused to take in the beauty of the blue, shadowed land that lay beneath her or the glitter of light about the house. It was still very early; we had not yet breakfasted; I was awake, with my arms upon the sill. Then she was gone, round the corner of the house, and I was retreating back across my room, fumbling in the sudden dark, and crossing

50

the creaking landing, and passing down the stairs on sandalled feet, my hand upon the banister, the hall below me crossed with light from a shutter that had swung open. I was in the hall, my hand upon the heavy latch, pushing up the wedge of wood, and her footsteps were reaching me, crunching as she came across the courtyard; I was the hostess, standing in the doorway at the top of the steps, shading my eyes against the morning glare, when one of the house cats came out to wind itself between my legs and watch with its narrowed pupils the approaching guest. A strange woman took off her dark glasses and said in a voice I did not know, 'Hallo. Sorry to arrive at this deathly hour. Can I come in?' I stared, but no trick of the light could make this woman into Anna, no thoughts came to make me understand. I said nothing for a moment, for I could not, literally, believe my eyes, and the woman said, beside me now, 'Yes, I know, it's a perfectly ghastly time to roll up, but I've been to collect my car. I wanted to be back in time for the class, but it took me less time than I'd thought it would. Sorry, let me introduce myself. I'm Jennifer Iliffe.'

'I'm Ruby Smith.' I had said it so often, during the past twenty-four hours, I felt I no longer knew that it was true. 'I'm sorry,' I said, 'It's just that I was expecting a friend.'

'Oh, I see. Did you think I was her?'

'Yes, I suppose I did. You're quite alike.'

'Oh, I've got hundreds of doubles. Everybody's always mistaking me for someone else, it happens all the time. I don't suppose it happens to you.'

'Do come in,' I said, 'I'll find some coffee. I expect

they'll be down soon. No, it doesn't happen to me. People just think I'm a half-caste or something. I'm sorry I was so rude, just staring like that.'

'That's all right,' she said, friendly, 'I told you, it's always happening. People stare at me in the street. They come up to me in shops sometimes and think I'm a relation of theirs. One man actually came up and hugged me from behind in the fish queue one day. He thought I was his wife.'

'It must be embarrassing. Cigarette? Sorry, I don't think the bread's arrived yet.'

'Thanks. Yes, it happened again on the way here, actually. In the garage. A man popped up beside me when I was talking to the mechanic about my car. Thought I was some girl he knew. He was frightfully apologetic. One can't help feeling sorry for disappointing people.'

'Still,' I said, 'for the people you know, you're the original, aren't you? All the others are the doubles.'

'Yes, I suppose that's something. I say, are you expecting your friend who looks like me to turn up here? That's going to be a bit confusing.'

I said, 'I was. Now, I don't think so. You see, the Fairbrothers thought you were her, too. But the point is, you aren't her; and if it's you that's here, then where is she?'

To worry about Anna, who was so calm, did not for some time occur to me; worry was for parents, for husbands, for people to whom unexplained absence was a threat, a blackmailing sentiment that was centred on the self. I could not say to Anna, 'I was worried about you.' But during that morning, the curiosity to know where she was grew into an agony

52

that I did not know; I was angry, too, that I had been left behind, duped again, allowed to wait and follow her and keep a rendezvous that she had not thought important; and anger feeds anxiety, anxiety strengthens anger. Turning myself at last to face my own needs, I knew that I must leave the painting school for my own reasons and search for Anna only so far as it suited me to do so. It is pure curiosity, I told myself, that will make me go to look for her; I buried fast the thought that I was too afraid to go on completely alone. France lay around me, no longer the land of infinite promise, but a large country fraught with dangers. The only sensible thing, after all, was to catch up with Anna so that we could continue our holiday as planned, spend the days sketching and exploring and our evenings in eating well, meeting together all the fascinating people whom, together, we could accept, losing ourselves in places which, for us together, held no terror. And at the end of the summer, there would be a store of experiences held in common, retold as the nightmares of childhood are retold in later life, with a laugh and a shrug, an exaggeration of the horror, because now all is safe. The solitary road, the single confrontation must lie forever in the mind, the road trod nightly in dreams, the meeting feared upon each street corner as the twilight comes. Then there is nobody to cling to, nobody to laugh, 'Do you remember?' no catharsis even, no relief. And so, although two stages on my journey were now past, I still decided to follow Anna, because when I found her we would laugh and mock ourselves and recreate in flippant mood each past event; because without her version I could not give

shape to my experience nor evaluate it. I was still no
nearer to discovering where she was, I sought with
undiminished eagerness, with the same desperation,
to find the whole picture in which she and I were
the figures, and still believed that one day I would
see it clear. There was the need, still keener now, to
find her, pin her down, demand of her 'What happened? What was it you saw that passed me by?' for
all my assumptions had been wrong. The Sandersons,
the Fairbrothers, all these people who should have
been a shared background to our outlined lives, all
faded into confusion, for they had been of no help.
'So, you got here at last?' The question rang in my
mind, mocking me. At last, at last; when should I get
there, when discover whether I was duped or loved,
when arrive and find an unequivocal greeting? Soon,
I said, soon; the pictures would move on, till, figures
and landscape passing on a screen, our little summer's life amused us when we sat in our deep arm-
chairs before a winter's fire. We would turn to each
other, smiling reminiscence. We would have grown
older painlessly. 'Where are you?' I demanded of her,
'and what is it that you have discovered? Give me a
clue, and I shall find the way.' But it was hard, in
these days of shifting impressions, to remember even
what her voice was like, it grew fainter, became a
caricature as I tried. I was shut out, because at last
I was not her, but I.

'Anna.' Had he spoken it in his sleep just now, or did
it simply tap in her head, a light hammer, urging her
to gather herself and go? There always were stains
on the walls of these hotel rooms, bloodstains where

54

other people killed mosquitoes. There always were mosquitoes, circling in darkness, their high-pitched landing whine. Silence was most ominous. After the silence, the blood one spattered upon the wall would be one's own. It was not possible still to be so alone. She lay, sweated, tossed her arms above her head, shook her hands around that warning whine, felt each inch of her body itch; and he lay there heavy as a bag thrown from a train that had landed for no reason in a certain spot, and never moved, but sometimes moaned and grunted. She stared, as the room lightened, at the back of a man's head, hair sticking upwards, shoulders hunched up smooth as chestnuts and the sheet falling away, private in sleep. Grey light came from a slit between the shutters, the room was coldly lit and she was cold suddenly beneath the sheets and hauled a slipping blanket back for cover. She saw her feet shine at the far end of the bed as if they had been cut off; curled her knees high to cover her cold extremities. Something stopped her still from moving closer, from stealing his warmth in sleep when it was impossible in waking. His flesh was warm, his back would thaw her like a radiator, his hands curled like a baby's would open easily if touched, would cover and stroke her cold limbs warm, his body turn will-less in sleep at a touch, to enclose her again in its life. Yet she shrank back and lay so far away from him that she almost tipped over the edge on to the floor, and fixed her eyes upon the ceiling to watch the changing patterns of light cast up from the street below. Now she wished that she had given him a false name, Prudence or Jennifer or Jane. Even Ruby would have done, for he would never have known; yet, no, 'I don't believe you,' he would have said; 'That's not your name, there is no glow, no Ruby red in you. Your feet touch mine on this August night like ice packs. You can't be Ruby.'

Now she pushed back the sheet and blanket and placed her feet upon the chill linoleum floor. Naked, seeing her long body like a wax candle, she was cold and ashamed, frightened too that he might awake and she not know what to say. Her clothes lay in a heap on a chair, slipping half to the floor, and she picked them out and put them on quickly, shivering as she fastened her bra, nearly falling as she balanced to put on her trousers yet saving herself with an outstretched hand to the wall. All the time he slept and did not move, and the light filled the room more solidly, filtered from the dawn outside. At last she took her bag from the corner behind the door and with a small click of the latch was gone without a backward look, her step light and quiet in the corridor, her head singing with the sounds released after controlled silence, her stomach sick with sleeplessness. In realising this eagerness to be gone, it was hard to remember why she had been there at all. There was still no consequence, no causality in her life; this she admitted once again, stepping from the hotel in the early dawn, leaving the bill unpaid, with detachment and not much surprise.

A poet with a poet's eyes. One could not help thinking at first, this man uses words to caress women, those he has loved lie naked on the open page for the world to see, like painters' mistresses, a hand covering the place. It made one wanton, indulging a new taste for self-exposure, it made one

56

want to delight and surprise, so that one would be remembered. It was hard to accept the absent-mindedness, the newspapers at breakfast, the casual reaching for a cigarette, and to stand about naked, only to be ignored. At first he had said 'You're beautiful' with a sigh that had given him at once what he wanted; beauty, she thought, a gift, it costs nothing, and since he would write of her she was proud to lie open to his gaze and then accept his slow exploring hand. There was a river at the bottom of the garden, that first morning, when she had made coffee. The night was over and it had all been quiet, ordinary, and nothing had happened, although she had hourly expected her bedroom door to open, after she had drunk wine with him that evening and seen his inquisitive look. Then there was morning, and they had come indoors from the river bank because there was a man working in a field on the horizon, and indoors, naked as children, self-conscious as if they had been in a play, they walked to the narrow sofa, pushed a lot of French magazines to the floor, and lay down. Shadow fell upon Anna like the cold of winter, moments afterwards where they lay, and chill struck upward from the cold floors.

'You can't be cold,' he said, 'it's about the hottest day of the year. And anyway, what am I for?' But soon he crossed the floor to get a drink, something ordinary, a glass of water and a cigarette where all should have been insubstantial as painted light. And she sat up, the hair falling about her shoulders to tickle up goose flesh upon her upper arms, and thought again how extraordinary men were, that they could switch so from one thing to another and not even feel the need to pretend.

'I must get dressed,' she said at last.

'Okay. I rather like the idea of staying like this.' A few drops, as she glanced, fell from him to mark the stone floor like perfunctory rain; she went past him, shielding herself, and he reached out and stared with a look that seemed to have little of poetry in it, and then sighed and dropped his arm and let her pass. Upstairs she washed in warm water and sat for a long time dreaming upon the bidet, and then brushed her hair, squeezed the last blobs of toothpaste from the tube, dropped the squashed thing into the plastic waste-paper basket; put on underwear and a light sleeveless dress, leaving arms and legs bare in order to seem friendly; and when she came back he wore his shorts and looked angry, a long glass of Pernod in his hand. Then he looked up, anger passing quickly as a cloud, and apologised, 'I like your dress,' telling her that even in clothes she was beautiful. And yet she was restless, uncomfortable, and turned away from his too close scrutiny.

She said, 'What about the sofa?' examining on the grey cushions a long, wet stain.

'It won't show.' He piled back the magazines and on the cover of the top one she saw advertised in French 'How the Frenchwoman chooses her lover for the holidays'; and knew that in giving herself to him so easily she had expected something particular in return. He was waiting for her here in this house; out of very kindness he was a poet; impatiently she went with him, wanting to be changed. And so the morning came, to leave, and he drove her car while she stared at his long hands upon the wheel, noticing

58

the white mark where a ring had been, his unknown, sharp-nosed profile cheating her of a full look at him for mile after mile. She did not really know where they went, the signs upon roads followed each other fast, landmarks she would have looked for passed unnoticed, churches where once she would have stopped to draw – on a hot afternoon, sketch pad and insect repellent, hat falling in curved shadow on the page – left like so many concrete boxes littering the land. Corners of fields, blond stubble stalks and Renoir poppies, river banks shaded with their dappling regiments of young poplars, were left untouched, as if they were scenery only and not the creations of masters. They ate meals together; and Anna, who would have paused to marvel and taste and comment on the wine, watched while he mixed everything together on his plate and dropped cigarette ash in it as he talked. Travelling with Ruby would have been so different; thinking this, she saw with irony her self easily changed, lightly blown aside; what one liked to think of as the reliable core of oneself, one's reaction to places, beauty, a field. or a church was as fickle as the rest then, could be discarded for the time being or told to wait in abeyance. Ruby would have been shocked, being not fickle but predictable. She thought of sitting with Ruby in a restaurant and the picture was absurd. 'What'll you have? I'm having the hors d'oeuvres.'

'Oh, the omelette, I think. It'd have the most marvellous ham in it, round here.'

'More wine? Oh, I can't think how one ever manages to do without it. Just think, eleven bob for that wretched Spanish burgundy that tastes of tin.'

'God, Anna, this is incredible. The taste of fresh basil, I'd forgotten it completely.'

'And tonight we'll be by the Loire. We can have fish, and one of those heavenly flowery white wines, and maybe rillettes or something delicious like that beforehand.'

But now she saw him drink Pernod with a crust of bread dipped into it, his food cooling before him because he 'didn't go wild about mixed up dishes'. She saw him in hotels pee in the bidet and lure cats across the roofs in the mornings to share his breakfast and lick up the precious white butter, she heard him in bars, his voice loud, struggling perfunctorily with the language, the hideous hybrid of his sentences, and guests looking away amused; she accompanied him and missed nothing, but still did not know what to say as she awaited with curiosity the pleasures that might be so much rarer, so much finer, that might change her utterly. It was easier, after all, to accept for a few minutes the thrust of a man's body in the act of love than to sit still and be easy while he trampled all uncaring on one's upbringing. Easier, yes; yet at times still infinitely hard, when he would sit up and look at her, apparently puzzled, with a slight frown as if in pain. Then he would say nothing for a while but go away and take a shower and sit down away from her, reading a book. 'What do you want me to do?' she wanted to say. But the words remained always unsaid, as if her lips would not release them. And then she cried without knowing why, for at other times, she said to herself, she had made other men happy; but her tears flowed without effort, soaking the sheet by her cheek, and they felt

60

meaningless in their spontaneity. He never turned to see her, but when she emerged at last dry and scrubbed from the shower he smiled friendlily as though nothing had happened, which indeed it had, and took her arm as they went downstairs. 'It is not my fault,' she told herself often, remembering that in relationships with men the whole concept of fault was out of date. 'It is not my fault.' She had to say it, though, to be exonerated. For in some things he was a child.

One day in a hotel room, when he was out, she looked through his things, out of idleness and curiosity but also from a deeper urge, since he evaded her and shook her off. It seemed, as all sins did, like asking for trouble, and she expected to find some small thing that would condemn her in her own eyes. For had they not decreed, she and Ruby, that this, and reading other people's letters, was the greatest treachery? It was in possessions that people were most vulnerable, objects left to scrutiny when the owner's back was turned. Coat collars revealed dandruff, stockings with holes in them unrolled themselves within drawers, desks bore bills, random jottings of thoughts best forgotten, there were things – the book of pornography under the bed, the bottle of emetic in the bathroom cupboard – that revealed needs both pathetic and obscene to the curious finder, showing a whole side of a person turned up unkindly to the light. But they were very few, this American's possessions in his small worn leather bag: a pair of old hairbrushes, English-looking, silver-backed, perfectly clean; a few clothes that had never been ironed but that nobody could be ashamed of; a diary with no entries in it, not a dentist appointment, not a secret rendezvous, not even crosses to mark the appointed days of a girlfriend's monthly period, but an address in New York which was presumably his own; packets and packets of American cigarettes. Then a small hard-backed book she picked out at last with relief and foreboding, thinking at least there is something; poems written neatly in crabbed biro, the words as squashed and squat, she thought as an anal obsessive's, each one copied yet smaller and blacker from a rough cast on the opposite page. She locked the door, sat down and began to read them carefully one by one, with less discernment of poetry than analytical, even medical care. He had found names for them to help her, giving a clue to each one's content to which to attach the found images. As she began, there was simple curiosity in her mind, then jealousy appeared, in case she might find some perfect woman spread there, looking out from where she lay at ease, through the windows of her home; but as she read on, bewilderment came to her, and irritation, and finally, as she looked up from the book and stared at the room about her, apathy. For they did not concern her, these poems, they had nothing direct to say to her, they held no clue as to whether she was right or wrong. They were written surely of another land and another time, a place in which death, not love, was the determinant and where men died pointlessly and were barely chronicled, but observed as if from a height as they twitched and were gone and others took their place. So she closed the book and put it away with the other things, and he came into the room much later, saying, 'What about

a walk before we eat? What about a drink, or shall
we see the church?' At dinner she watched his hands
spread on the red chequered tablecloth and his eyes
following the waiter's movements and the coming
and going of other customers, as if he waited for a
cue; she saw that he was nervous, tapping his fork
upon the cloth, tipping a wine glass to and fro to
watch the running purple wine. Afterwards they
stood at the doorway and saw the moon, an exact
half, veined like Roquefort, stuck up there above the
houses. He sighed and said that he was tired, as if
they had been together long enough to say that, and
she, solicitous of weakness, ran a hand across the
back of his neck where the hair grew long and soft
and was darker than his bleached crown, and suggested that they go to bed; and his flesh seemed to
quiver and shrink under her touch, as if he were cold,
or perhaps afraid of her, or perhaps even like some
men and dogs disliked to be touched just there,
among the hackles. Under the yellow light of the
little hall at the stairway, his face looked to her pale,
older than she had seen it. He paused and turned to
her as if he would say something in a moment, but
then the concierge crossed the hall to her desk and
looked at them both so that Anna, panicking, felt
herself fixed there, photographed by the woman's
assessing eyes, and he moved on without speaking,
his hand large and heavy and slow on the banisters,
his weight upon the stairs heard with each step. It
was this night, as it grew pale at its other extremity,
that she got up in the dawn and went away, to leave
him sleeping, as they say, like a child. And crossing
the bald grey square outside while the whole town

slept on, she congratulated herself with each spring-
ing step on having made a decision.

'Aigues-Mortes,' Anna said to me before she left,
'if it's simply awful, let's go to Aigues-Mortes.' We
chose the name for its resonance from among the
towns of the Rhône delta; I saw in my mind a city
of bones, bleached against a Mediterranean purple
sky. 'The Camargue should be good,' she said,
'Lovely light, lots to paint. Don't you think?'
I said, 'If it's not cluttered up with tourists lump-
ing about on horses in sky-blue slacks.'
And she said, 'Damn the tourists. One can always
get away.' I wanted, without admitting it to her, to
see the church at Les Saintes-Maries de la Mer,
where a black virgin, I am told, stands in the crypt,
the gypsies' saint; and so, we will stay in Aigues-
Mortes, we said, if it is awful, and in this way provided ourselves with an escape. Now I spread my
map upon my bed, my finger upon the ringed place
that marked the painting school, and saw the roads
stretch away in all directions, the road back to the
place where Anna had sent her postcard, the road
forward to the south and the sea. Aigues-Mortes, a
finger pointing into the sea, looked like an end, a
destination. To arrive there would be some kind of
achievement, and I could, if she were still not there,
light my candle at the gypsies' shrine without risking
her sarcasm. I was nearly sure, though, I saw her in
my mind following the road that I had taken, a few
days only in advance of me; I smiled to think of her
making the same decisions, flying from the Fairbrothers in her usual fastidiousness, assuming once

64

again the strength of the telepathy between us that would allow me to follow and find her, after no word of explanation.

'I knew you'd come on here,' she would say, airily certain of the rightness of her own reaction. 'I knew you'd loathe it as much as I did.' And we would stroll out into the streets of Aigues-Mortes, light-hearted, liking ourselves in our freedom from conventional bonds and explanations. 'I can't see the point of putting up with something you don't like,' Anna would say, she who was always walking out of cinemas halfway through films, while I, who felt some obligation to stay to the end, if I had paid to do so, would join her in the street with a laugh of relief, 'Yes, it was bad, wasn't it?' and stifle my curiosity to know the end, however pointless it might be.

'I knew you were bored stiff,' she would say, and I, who had not had time to discover my true feelings, would agree.

And now she had to be in Aigues-Mortes because it had been her idea, and she must vindicate it. Dismiss it she might, once I was there, with a light 'God, I can't think why we came to this place,' but go there she must, for however short a time, until I could arrive and see her used to it. There would be a particular café, where the wine was better than anywhere else, a certain little restaurant where one could eat sea food so cheaply, a *pâtisserie* that sold the best cakes, a point on the ramparts at which she had found her favourite view; by the time I had arrived, she would have established all this, as if she had lived there for years, and yet as soon as I joined in and began to play the game too, it would be time for her to leave. And by then something would have happened that showed us how right we were to leave, how skilfully we in our intuition had chosen the right moment. I recognised this pattern in my life, yet could not resent it, for this was how things had always been, ever since those two children we had been began to grow up.

There was mist on the hills and hanging down in wisps over patches of road, as I drove away from Saint-Louis, and for an hour or so I kept the enclosed feeling that it gave me, the certainty that nobody could see what I was doing. The Fairbrothers had been as easy to leave as to greet; vague, friendly, insulting, forgetting one's name. Upon their egotism, I felt, the names and faces of others could never make more than the faintest of impressions, so that it was unsurprising that their children had that lost and startled look, like orphans. I thought of Tamsin as I drove, and tried to imagine a lifetime of trying to make some impression on Kirstin; there are ways of infanticide more brutal than those of the Spartans, there are ways of cancelling people, of denying them life, that do not occur to one until one sees the victim, the lost eyes mindlessly following another's movement. I was glad, glad enough to be excited, that I had escaped and was once more alone upon the road, and I sang, and the mist parted upon high blue sky.

It was towards midday that I stopped at a roadside café, sure enough of myself to pause and sit down alone, my map and my Michelin guide beside me, and ask for coffee.

'I'm very sorry,' the man at the bar said, 'we have no coffee, Madame. It is a little late. You should perhaps have come earlier. A drink, yes.'

Slightly shaken from my composure, I stared at the row of bottles behind him, unable to decide. The bottles looked criminal, half full as they were of unknown dark liquids, their labels old and stained; as if they were absinthe, or worse, and would blind or petrify me or carry me straight upon the streets. If I had been with a man, it would have been easy to assent to one or other of the suggestions the barman made. 'Anis, Madame? Or an aperitif? Saint-Raphael, perhaps? Byrrh? Cognac? Or, you are English, you prefer to drink beer?' But I was alone, I faltered and shook my head and said at last, 'A glass of wine, please.'

'Ah, a glass of wine. Red or white, Madame?'

'Red, please. And have you,' I looked about for signs, 'anything to eat?'

'A sandwich, Madame? Ham, pâté, cheese.'

'Oh, pâté. A pâte sandwich, please, and a glass of wine.' I hovered near the bar, hunting in my bag for a cigarette.

'Won't you sit down, Madame?' He indicated a chair set alone at a little table, a dark bentwood chair, its seat polished by hundreds of bottoms. Without looking at any of the others who stood around the bar, whose gaze I felt curiously upon me, I went straight across and sat down. The men at the bar muttered and turned their backs again, crowding together until they were one blue hunched shape, their broad shoulders under their workmen's clothes, their heads of black crisp hair under berets tilted to hear the latest jokes at the barman's expense. I looked at their red sunburnt necks above their collars, heard

their bawdy laughter and the soft occasional lines of
song, and thought how easily, how carelessly, men
everywhere make themselves exclusive. Their wives
would be at home, stirring great pots in the steam of
raftered kitchens, holding the purse strings, exerting
their wills, while the men loitered and laughed here,
and clapped each other on the back, calling each
other 'tu' with the softness of lovers, playing like
boys from school once the releasing bell has been
rung. Watching them, I felt myself an anomaly; I
drank up my wine as quickly as I dared and nervously longed to leave. And then the plastic strips
that hung over the doorway were shivered again,
with a noise of aspen leaves in the wind, and the
light broke up differently, for somebody else was
coming in – a tall man who went straight to the
bar, yet had to hover on the edge of the crowd, a
stranger like me. The men half-turned, moved a little
to accommodate him, but because he was a man too,
were hardly disturbed. I saw the patches of dark
sweat on the back of his blue shirt, the dust staining
his trouser legs. His light hair, plastered down by a
swift hand before entering, curled darker with sweat
at his neck, long and sleek. He stood on one leg like
a horse resting, and leaned upon a small strip of the
bar between other men's elbows and asked rather
loudly, in bad French, for a Pernod; and was served
without a word, but with a smile half-friendly, half-
wary. Lost, with his glass, he stood for a moment and
looked about helplessly for somewhere to stand or
sit. His case, battered leather covered with labels and
the white dust of the road, stood propped by the
door. At last there was a stool in the corner and he

crossed with a long stride to sit upon it, his arms
stretched out across the table before him as if to cool
on the welcome chill metal, his tall glass of cloudy
liquid in front of him, a cigarette raised frequently
to his mouth. He glanced at me and I at him; then
in self-protection I took off the glasses I wear for
driving and put them on the table and glancing back
saw only a blur of brown and blue. He crossed before
me, with his empty glass, to return to the bar and
say something to the barman; I could not hear above
the laughter of the others, the shouts as a small man
downed another cognac, what it was he said; but I
saw the outline of his hands making shapes in the air,
pointing with a flung out gesture in the direction of
the road. The barman listened, nodded, banged upon
the bar top, making the glasses jump.

'Anybody here going to Aigues-Mortes?' he
shouted. 'Any of you blokes going that way?'

There was a second's silence, then they all began
to talk at once and flip at each other with their broad
hands. 'This fellow wants a lift,' the barman shouted;
and they all turned to shout back to the barman, then
to the young traveller, emphatic, serious and gesticu-
lating, yelling to where the younger man stood as if
being foreign he must be deaf. He put up his hands to
his face and smiled his protest. With my glasses once
more upon my nose, I saw his smiling, embarrassed
brown face, the tiredness of his eyes.

'Nîmes? Nîmes any good? I'm going down to
Nîmes,' one of the *camion* drivers said, waving a
hand to silence the others. 'That any good? It's not
far along the coast from there, not really, and there's
plenty of traffic on the coast road.'

'Nîmes.' The young man frowned, not knowing, and appealed to the barman once again.

'Well, I'm bound for Aigues-Mortes itself,' another man interrupted, quieter, the stub of a Gauloise stuck to his lip, 'Eventually, that is. I've got to go via Alès and Arles. That any good for you, Monsieur?'

The young man smiled and began to thank him in his bad French, and all the drivers, delighted, began to laugh and exclaim 'Sure thing' and 'Okay, baby' and 'President Nixon – pooh!' slapping each other and roaring their pleasure. The American stood rather helpless, and smiled still, and placed his glass upon the counter, and dropped his cigarette to the floor.

'Come on then, mate,' the fat man who was driving him exclaimed, 'Let's be off. I've been here an hour or two too long already.' He led the way out, calling back, 'Salut, Maurice!' cuffing a couple of friends who stood about in his way, flipped aside the plastic strips of curtain with a flourish. The American following him with a shy hand raised for good-bye was a thin and insubstantial figure beside the glistening fat and hairiness of the driver; but his eyes, as they passed over me in a brief glance as he went out, were brilliant and struck with surprise. I heard the slamming of doors and the deep throaty engine starting, and a grinding of wheels as the *camion* turned. For a moment its bulk blocked the light as it backed towards the café door; departing, it left a brief blast of wind to lift the curtains and rattle them again. In a moment or two I got up and paid for my drink, took my sandwich, uneaten and wrapped in thin paper, and started off on the road again, still alone.

70

It is odd that after so short a time one can forget the original meaning of one's actions; alone, one passes the point of self-justification and begins to act instinctively. To somebody – to John, I think – I had said so recently, 'Of course it's the travelling that matters. One goes abroad for the journey, not for arriving anywhere in particular.' And John – it was John – had said, 'Well, I'm flying. I think it's where you're going that matters. I want to get there as quickly as possible.' And I did not reply, 'Well, you'll be on your honeymoon,' not wanting to inflict further embarrassment, but said only, rather superciliously, 'We all have different reasons.'

It was Anna who said, 'Marvellous to think of travelling again, isn't it, after this ghastly winter. Huddling by one's fireside, hardly daring to go out. God, the open road, I can hardly wait. It's the only thing that really makes me feel free. Not knowing where one's going to spend the next night. Not planning. Not having to do anything you don't want to.' And it was I who agreed. Now I had closed my mind, it seemed, to all except catching up with her. I fought my sense of failure, my inability to offer that young man a lift; I drove on despising myself for having given something up, refusing to admit the voice that told me, 'Well, you were wrong, weren't you? You don't like travelling, you're afraid of it.' Refusing to go slow.

Moissac was past, the Arab curves of the great church door I had promised myself, the cloister where the secrets are carved. It was as if I had passed a shrine, forgetting my pilgrimage, confined to the square container of metal that carried me on; dust-stained, angry, a twentieth-century traveller denying herself the cool drink by the wayside that makes the journey possible, I hurried to my objective; a modern pilgrim foregoing the caress of the saint's hand, averting my eyes from the crowds that queue for blessing. For places, stillness, the stone men of earlier centuries console me; forbidding myself that consolation, because I dared not stop, I saw only the dipping road, the dusty wayside grass, trampled in summer. Albi's tall red cathedral caught my eye only as I waited in a traffic jam, the steepness a walled labyrinth, the brick like sunset. I saw a wedding party come out, the bride a white butterfly fluttering at the base of the wall, the men in black like gardeners, tidying the crowd. Cameras flashed in the hands that held them, the bridal couple's smile held fast against the bland wall, while I watched for a moment, and was herded on. A little bridesmaid ran down the steps and was pulled back to stand in line. Through the open doors, joining with the noise of the traffic, the organ music broke loose like the voice of God bellowing, but the couple never faltered, never trembled, but stood smiling after an ordeal. In a café on a corner, as I turned towards the south beneath a policeman's waving white hand, I saw Henri de Toulouse-Lautrec, his black beard jutting, crouched to observe, a gnome with a huge glass in his hand. But the city, like other cities, was past before it had seen me; I was a fly crawling among flies upon its wall, leaving no trace. Without having spoken a word, I was through it and away again, dazzled at my impudence, and the treasures of the place were still dust-covered, sheeted, put away. Nothing is demanded of one. It is all very simple. Driving on is like waking from a dream one has forgotten. One thinks, maybe one day it will return.

By evening, then, I was upon the spit of land that runs along beside the sea, a ribbon placed there that in a moment might be blown away, with the dry shifting sand and the light little cardboard-box hotels that have been dropped along the way. A child has been playing with egg boxes, has spent a bored afternoon painting lurid signs; all the litter and clutter along the sea front will be tidied up in a minute by a strict mother and put away for the night, so that only the moon and the dark straight sea-line are left, and the lights upon the water are the lights from the stars. Paper blowing across the road, dancing into the wheels of my car, is crushed and flattened. There are dry sandy people coming up from the beach, parched and brown as if from the desert, their eyes washed pale by the sun's brilliance. Tired children trail along and are caught fiercely by the hand, lined up before they cross the road. I am reminded of puppets that will not be still, their dry wooden stick-jointed legs. There is a weariness under the metallic sky, even the brownish sand, stuck with old tins and bottles and sodden paper, has been trodden and turned endlessly, and is exhausted. I think of the smooth stone faces of the medieval men I did not see this time at Moissac, how their features are unchangeable so that they are everyone at once, because nothing can touch them. No blowing air, no paper, no casual touch of hands can wear them out. They are deliberate in stone, and inexhaustible. Here I drive with my sense

of an irreparable loss, along the road where the tar-
mac is patched and rutted, soft and black in the sun,
and nothing seems deliberate. Chance has thrown
these places together and chance, like the puff of
breath from an irresponsible god, will blow them
away.

But the stones, the towers of Aigues-Mortes are
before me, the colour of a winter evening sky; and
in a moment I am turning in through the gateway
that announces me like a dignitary arriving, so that I
am somebody, I have entered, making a choice; the
soldiers on the ramparts have spied me and there is
no turning back. Only the cold sea when the sun has
left it, washing far from the stranded walls, comes
and goes. The town is laid out before me in neat
squares, so that all choices are equal. Its grid gives
me the chance to go everywhere, yet gives me no
clue where to start. I park my car in the square and
see the streets go off at right angles all around me,
and other streets, narrower, at right angles to them.
The whole pattern is enclosed by the great grey
walls. My problem is set out for me here, clear as an
intelligence test, defined by the limits of the city
walls. I set out, walking, to look for the hotel.

'Miss Anna Parrish.' The woman repeated it carefully, the weight of her voice falling on the last syllables. 'Non, Mademoiselle, there was nobody of that
name. You see, we have the *fiches*, it is a police rule.
That way we know who is here.'

'Oh, well. Thank you. But you do have a room for
the night? Just for one, that is. And I would like
dinner and breakfast, if it's possible.'

74

'Yes, Mademoiselle, that is possible. May I show you the room? This way, up the stairs, please.'

I stood on the landing. 'I would like a room at the back, if possible.' Outside, lorries and motor cycles churned up the narrow street, horns hooted and men bellowed to each other. My mind was tired out with the effort of driving. She was already unlocking a door, showing me a bare clean room, a bed with a pink satin counterpane and a window that was shuttered to the street, filtering in light and noise. 'At the back? This is the best room, though. Here you have the sun, and the bed is best. But still,' as I hesitated, stood there unconvinced, 'If you want a room at the back, wait just a moment, Mademoiselle, if you don't mind, and I will fetch the key.' She had to go downstairs to get the key for the back bedroom, and I waited on the landing, looking out through the small window on to red roofs and the setting sun. The key turned in the lock, the dark woman glanced at me and pushed open the door. Inside, the room was dark, the shutters closed. The air was stale and hot; Madame strode across the room and threw the shutters open, exclaiming, 'You are English, you like fresh air,' and I put down my suitcases and sat upon the mountainous bed, smiling my acceptance.

'Dinner will be ready for you, Mademoiselle.' She left me, her backward glance anxious for a moment, and I sat looking at my surroundings. The bed dipped, so that it was easy to roll back into its hollow. I lay, looking up at the huge wardrobe, the heavy ugly mantelpiece and the square of hardboard tacked over the fireplace. Below the window, in a little square of concrete yard, there was a clatter of metal, as if somebody were dragging a lawn mower. She was right, the other room had been more pleasant; but it seemed to be too late now to change my mind. And as I crossed the landing to go downstairs, my strange back room became all at once a prize, as I heard Madame, at the bar, tell a person who stood out of sight, 'I'm sorry, Monsieur, but the back room is taken. We have a room at the front that is free, and I do not think you will be disturbed.'

The man's voice fumbled with his answer, in schoolboy French, and I heard again the clink of the keys taken down from their hook; but it was only as I stood flattened against the wall to let them pass that I knew the man from the café, the American who had hitched a lift. He passed very close to me, following Madame up the dark winding stair and across the narrow landing, and I smelt sweat as he passed and saw his eyes flicker up briefly to meet mine, his lips move to murmur, 'Bonjour, Madame'. I could not tell, from his politeness, if he had remembered me, and was surprised that he spoke to me in French. He was taking the front room, the one with the rose-coloured counterpane. I heard the springs creak as he threw his case upon the bed, and Madame, in her clacking cork-soled mules, came down the stairs. She glanced at me. 'C'est un Américain.' Thinking, no doubt, that I was a fool to let a man, an American, take the best room. 'Ah, oui?' I replied. And descended the stairs behind her, in silence.

In my effort to assimilate what is happening, I hold imaginary conversations, with a recipient of my version whom I think is Anna.

'And so I took the back room, and, wasn't it an extraordinary coincidence, that young man, you know, the one in the café, the one who wanted a lift to Aigues-Mortes, he arrived only about half an hour after me, and came to the same hotel and said he'd have the front room. Isn't it extraordinary, how things . . .' In the same way I write letters in my head, changing my perception to fit the reader's, so that what I say may seem acceptable. But there is no answering consciousness. Nobody exclaims with enthusiasm, 'God, how extraordinary, and d'you know what happened to me – ?' There is nobody to tear open the letter, eager to know how I saw it, making my vision true because it is seen, read, taken in. Something is not working. There is a reluctance somewhere to say what I saw, what I did. Either I am lying, or the other does not believe me. I consider the scene, that night, the next morning, the next few days. 'Anna, I must tell you – ' But no, I do not want to tell, that is it; not to say, I thought, I felt this. There is a reluctance, because something has intruded which is not a part of my picture of myself; an unknown, a delicate thing which I do not yet even want to express nor try to fit too definitely into the picture. And yet, I see what is happening. It is strong, clear in my mind, coloured under the acid light of the Mediterranean sun. It is there, all right. It happened, I am sure. And so I try again.

There are a few people in the wide sunny room where breakfast is served in the mornings, but there is the smell of coffee newly ground and brewed, there is blue smoke rising from a cigarette, and upon the bar-top a box full of bread that has just arrived, brought in by a hurried young man in blue overalls. The tables that last night were littered with carafes of wine, fragments of bread and the fat spilt from plates of food set down hastily, are clean and bare. Two or three are set with checked tablecloths and little plastic baskets holding a few slices of bread. Another is spread with the morning's papers, laid flat like a deck of cards. An old man sits in one corner and a small white jug of coffee, a smaller jug of milk, are brought in and set before him. He takes a slice of bread and breaks it, dipping it into the shallow cup, sucking the coffee from it through the gaps in his teeth. He was in this corner last night and sits there still, his blue shirtsleeves rolled above hairy, tattooed forearms, the veins protuberant on the soft inner flesh; as if he has not moved all night, but has sat there while the crumbs and debris are cleared around him, as if he has been dusted and straightened and left where he is. At another table, facing towards the door, a young man sits, waiting for his pots of coffee and milk. When they are brought, he asks for jam and butter and looks around him nervously, and tucks the corner of the large checked napkin into his shirt-neck for something to do. There is a woman sitting at a table on the opposite side of the room, her back to the wall, and he has smiled at her once or twice, has said, 'Good morning,' in a murmured tone as he entered the room, but he has not spoken further. He smiles distantly to her as he begins his breakfast, as if he waited for her approbation to begin. She nods to him, maintaining the distance, and then looks

78

away, pretending to stare anxiously towards the kitchen, as if she is in a hurry and cannot wait longer for her breakfast. When the steaming jugs are set before her, she is gracious to the woman who brings them, and says, 'How delicious,' before she begins to pour her coffee and spread butter upon her bread. There is a silence in the room like the silence in trains that are mysteriously held up; in a moment, if the train does not move, strangers will begin to speak to each other, emphasising the nuisance of the delay; if it does move on, they will sigh and exclaim with relief and settle back after a minute or two into their own thoughts. Only the old man in the corner relaxes in the silence, being insulated from the other passengers; he is the guard, or the man who is always there, who expects the delay and is unsurprised. He does look round, though, stirring from his immobility, when the glass door swings open and a policeman strides across the room, barely pauses to greet anyone, and knocks once or twice upon the bar counter. A policeman wearing a cape, although it is hot outside, and a little peaked cap; he has a dark moustache and is jerky, like a policeman in an old film. He shouts, 'Madame! Est-ce que Madame Devrier est là?' and the woman, plump and dark in her apron, wiping her hands, a creased frown between her brows, stands impatiently before him, giving him grudgingly a minute of her time. I am a busy woman, I have lunch to prepare, her stance says, I have no time for fiddling around with police matters. The policeman asks to see her husband, and her frown deepens. 'Impossible, Monsieur. He is not here, he is asleep.' The old man who last night, the woman remembers, was addressed more than once as *le patron*, sits still in his corner, his eyes bright and lidded like a lizard's, watching. The policeman is trying to make her go to wake her husband, but Madame Devrier refuses, her arms coming up to express outrage, the preposterous idea. 'Why can't you speak to me?' she is demanding, 'Why can't you tell me whatever it is you have to say?' The policeman looks around the room, sees two foreigners and an old man still as stone, and turns back to the woman. She is telling him, he can come into the kitchen for a minute, but that she has little time to waste. He pushes up the flap of the bar, closes it again carefully behind him, looks again at the three in the sunny room, and follows Madame Devrier into the kitchen. The young man, lighting a cigarette, raises his eyebrows at the young woman, who is still slowly chewing her bread and jam, and she glances back at him with a slight grimace of recognition, surprise, amusement. He says at last, in a loud voice, daring to break the silence now that the accident has taken place, 'Well, what was all that about?'

She shrugs slightly, raises her brows, 'Goodness knows.' She is curious, but fears to be told. The old man from his corner says indistinctly, 'C'est-ce qu'il y avait un mort, vous voyez.'

'Un mort?' The young man looks wildly across at the girl, 'That means a murder, doesn't it?'

'Just somebody dead,' she replies. 'Comment,' she asks the old man, enunciating clearly as if this will make him speak clearly back. 'Il y avait un mort ici?'

He mumbles to her that this is so, and for a moment his eyes gleam as if he will tell her the whole story, but Madame Devrier enters, brisk and angry, to clear away the cups and saucers, and he changes his mind, gets up from the table with one eye upon her and moves out through the glass door into the sunshine. The young man and the young woman watch Madame as she moves about, clearing away the crockery, as they wait to be told more.

'C'était la police,' she says eventually, and their eyes are blank, expectant. She goes on to say that the police are a meddlesome lot of time-wasters and that she has no truck with them, and as for expecting her to wake her husband at this hour, and as for striding into the kitchen and making her soup curdle with their nonsense, and as for wasting honest people's time, they have not enough to do, they can't busy themselves stopping all these revolutions but have to come barging into her kitchen, and at this hour. Then she is gone, dumping her pile of crockery, turning on the tap at the bar hard so that the froth rises, and bubbles appear in the air, and break gently upon the bar counter, and she is shouting to somebody in the back yard, somebody called Pierre, to hurry up and fetch the fish. The young man sighs and says to the girl across the tables that separate them, 'Well, I guess that's one thing we'll never know.' They are together here for a moment, left alone in the room, hovering behind their tables now that breakfast is finished, uncertain whether to move towards each other more surely; but the girl shakes herself, un-friendly after a bad night, says that she must go out and do some shopping, and he accepts this and does not offer to accompany her. From the whitewashed hotel they go different ways down the street, walking away from each other along the narrow pavement where the shadow falls like a blade from jutting roofs.

At the corners of the street, both turn, pause for a second, wondering which way to go, and as the girl sees the man take the road to the left, she takes hers to the right, continuing up towards the square while he walks towards the sea. But because it is laid out in rectangles, because the permutations of streets, as they cross each other and cross again, are infinite, they move restrictedly, like figures upon a chess board, avoiding the same square. She moves up a street into the blazing sun of the open square, and crosses the square, looking about her, her eyes shaded, and walks towards a building at the far corner. He turns back from the rampart wall and looks about him and decides on a dark alleyway where only cats and children sit and look at him, and goes up it towards a building on its corner where there are men sitting under an awning playing cards. She enters the building she has reached, going up two whitened steps into a dark room, the windows curtained with growing greenery so that inside it is like an aquarium. He enters his building, and finds a billiard table and a fat woman knitting at a counter. Presently both emerge, and set off again, right and left and right again, following the patterns of the streets, their eyes drawn by random objects but always seeking the most likely, the most promising place. She walks determinedly down a street where there are shops on one side, selling straw hats and french beans and bursting red peppers, and on the other side, two hotels next to each other. She pushes the hanging curtain in the first doorway aside, and is

82

just inside when she sees the young man leap like a
cat down the steps of the one next door and pause in
the street for a moment, with the puzzled, wrinkled
face of an animal that has lost a scent; then he is
turning to the hotel where she stands, about to come
in, to push back the curtain with a brown hand, to
walk into the half-light and discover her. She is
alone in the foyer, she has not yet rung the bell and
no concierge, no plump knitting figure is there to
receive her; she opens a door and steps into a telephone kiosk, her back turned to the foyer, her head
bent, and pretends to be making a call. She is sure
now that he is following her. The young man enters,
pushing aside the curtain, is across the foyer in three
steps, and stands at the desk, his finger hovering over
the brass push-button bell. The bell rings. A woman
comes out from a back room, thin and hurried, pushing back her hair. He asks her questions, waving his
hands in the air, his face contorting with the unruly
words. She listens, lips drawn together, and then
opens a book and looks down a page, her finger
marking the way. She shakes her head, and will hear
no more; she is certain. He droops, his fatigue all at
once apparent, and walks slowly back towards the
door, while the girl in the telephone box turns
quickly away and fiddles with money in her bag.
When the concierge has returned to her room, and
the curtain over the door no longer swings with the
impact of the man's departure, she comes out, blink-
ing, into the white street, and stands for a moment
on the pavement, watching him move away on his
slow, pacing stride. She pauses, fear clouding her
mind after this morning's event like a small shadow

passing across water; and then she shoulders her bag
and walks, swift and determined, after him up the
street.

Yes, the clear vision I seek moves, I suppose,
like this. An impersonal eye surveys the scene. We
move, and something records our presence and our
vacillations, as the quivering pencil of a cardiograph
traces the beating of a heart, the filling of a lung. I
think of the charts fixed over the cots of newborn
premature babies; the babies sleep and are unconscious, their limbs twitch, and it is all recorded. The
places where we move about are drawn and drawn
upon, become a palimpsest. All of us meet at this
spot, where once we stood; all of us interlock. The
streets, the corridors are thronging with us, the patterns repeat again and again. Now I see the record
and wonder what it was that moved, causing it.
Figures move, the line moves trembling up and
down; but I cannot just watch it, entranced; I must,
I suppose, admit to feeling something, to being in-
volved. In a busy street in a foreign town, I saw, as
I say, the departing back of a man in a bright blue
shirt, and there was something already familiar about
the shape of his head, the movement of his shoulders
as he walked; something that made me start after him,
shaking myself free of apprehensions, and pursue him
along the way he had gone. Something impelled
me to go on, to follow him, to force an explanation. I
go back, searching, to the morning of that strange day.

It was odd to have slept so badly, when the room
was quiet and I tired after my journey. I remember
this surprise, this waking irritable. And the previous
evening, my conversation with the *patronne*, when I

84

had gone down in my dressing-gown and found her in the kitchen and asked for a brandy to help me sleep.

She said, friendly, 'Are you on holiday alone, then?'

And I told her, 'I am looking for a friend. She should have been here, in this hotel, but you have not seen her.'

'I hope you find her then, Mademoiselle.'

'Yes, so do I. After a bit, you don't know where to look. You're so sure you will find the person, it seems too surprising when you don't. We were to have met at a painting school in the Lot valley. But she wasn't there, so I came on here, which was our next meeting place, as it were.'

'But why Aigues-Mortes particularly?'

'Oh,' I said, 'the Camargue. You must get a lot of tourists, don't you? We wanted to paint. And it's such an extraordinary name.'

'Yes, an extraordinary name. Well, I hope you find your friend. There was a man here, looking for his wife. She, too, should have been in Aigues-Mortes.'

'A man?' I almost expected to hear now that Anna had been secretly married.

'A German.'

'Oh. Did he find her?'

'No, Mademoiselle, he did not.' She turned back to polish the glass and poured a measure of brandy for me. 'There you are. It's good for the digestion, good for the liver. Well, I hope you sleep well, Mademoiselle. It's going to be a good day tomorrow, you must go to the beach.'

'Good night, Madame,' I said, and went like a child in my dressing-gown, holding my nightcap, a tumbler of brandy to drink alone in a hotel room, as if this place had been waiting for me. I switched on the bedside light and the room was patched only with darkness, the great wardrobe a wall with the unknown lurking behind it, the shutter a crack open to let in the night air. I heard the clock across the square strike midnight, and switched off my light for my eyes strained after the signs upon the page and found them indecipherable. The big lumpy bed stretched around me so that my hands and feet must make a cold and alarming journey to find the far extremities; I came to an edge shaking with achievement and dared not turn back to find the other, but tucked the duvet in a lump behind my back, as if it were another person, and lay staring into the darkness. Red coils and blue spines invaded my eyes; I saw only my inner eye, and the true darkness was impenetrable. There was only a whole great room around me, full of furniture, and I could see none of it. Something could move out from behind the wardrobe, some slimy unimaginable object could descend slowly from the ceiling; any kind of appalling creation could converge on me, and I would not know. Blind, bandaged with darkness, I would be helpless. This was the first time on my sunlit journey that the unknown had appeared to me as terrible, as dark and threatening. I switched on the light, scrabbling to find the cord, press the plastic, and I was again in a circle that cleared of blame the bed, the floor near me and part of the carpet; but the outer darkness was still there, yet more hostile now because it was partly seen, the outline of chair, wardrobe and desk clear against the wall, the dark concavities merely guessed at, the other side always unknown. Forced by some dawning knowledge of a new fear, I switched the light off again; for the complete ignorance of total darkness could never be worse than a hint, a clue. If something were there that threatened me, I did not want to know. I closed my eyes and mind and thought of the green fields of France through which I had come to this time and place, and in a few minutes was asleep.

But an hour or so later I was awake again, and seized by a terror that I knew in childhood, by a part of my eight-year-old self, a person long forgotten. Not since then, that particular holiday in a rented house by the sea in England, had I experienced this – my own, my familiar horror. And now it came flooding back over me, stronger than memory, stronger than consciousness, a fear that meant paralysis and the drying of all mucus and saliva so that face and body became stiff, corpse-like, a chill that spread from motionless feet and grew, cold fingers moving up the legs, the thighs finally paralysed, cold as death, the terror moving slowly towards the heart. I have to write it this way, I have to see a nameless and unknown victim, for otherwise I am forced to see myself gripped by this little death, myself reflected in a mirror as I grimace and writhe away, trying to escape; myself ludicrously transfixed by fear. The victim, the other, allows me to go free from this childish absurdity, this simple fear of the dark; so I write it clinically. I could not stretch a hand out to switch on my bedside light again, but lay, my breathing very shallow, knowing now, at twenty-eight, what I did not know at eight; that if I lay and accepted it all, taking it 'in, knowing through every pore the extent of my

fear, only then would it recede. Like pain, like ebb-
ing water, the terror withdrew, and I, recently only
the victim, lay a beached wreck upon the sand, upon
the ribbed solid land where the waves had washed
and washed, and shuddered my relief. The darkness
was again cool, exterior, lying close againt my flesh
yet not invading it; the centre of my mind had let it
in, opening the flood gates, and it had come in and
been there and finally receded. For the last few hours
of that short summer night I slept again.

Morning sun was painful upon the eyes, the fierce
single beam of an optician's torch. I blinked and
shrank from it, as if the hours of darkness had not
been long enough. It was I who stood in the street,
not the other, not the victim; who watched the
American walk away and was dizzy with tiredness.
My hand reached for the rough white surface of a
wall to steady me, and the town with its mounting
noise of traffic and increasing vigour of buying and
selling, had me trapped in its labyrinth, a squared
and regular maze that would not let me go. I walked
in a straight line down the street after him, choosing
to be the follower rather than the followed. When I
reached a corner and paused again, not knowing
which way to go, I saw him sitting at a café table on
the opposite corner, and it was too late to return
again to the shadows.

He raised his head and smiled at me, and waved
his hand, as if he had known anyway that I would
appear.

'Good morning again. Will you come and join me
in a drink? You must be needing one by now.'

I stood in hesitation at the kerb, and he gestured to the boy who was serving drinks. The boy, dark and crop-haired, stood in attention beside the table, his tray drooping from his curled brown hand.

'I'll have a Pernod,' the American said in his flattened French. And waited, looking at me.

I stood there still. 'All right. A cognac, please. And a glass of water.'

'Won't you sit down?'

I did, scraping the metal legs of the chair upon the stone, folding my hands before me on the warm tin top of the table.

'And a cognac and a glass of water.' The boy strolled off to the bar, polished two glasses on a white cloth and set them upon the tray. The Beatles sang through the crackling radio. We were silent, waiting for our drinks. Men in the shady interior flipped through packs of cards, brought the palms of their hands down with a smack upon the table, exclaimed and protested, the cards fluttering through their hands and falling. The American handed me my tiny glass with its gold rim and the brandy pale as china tea, and poured water into his own glass until it became opaque.

'Having a good time?' he asked me.

'What do you mean?'

'Well, your holiday. Don't say you aren't here on holiday. So I hope you're having a good time.'

'Yes, thank you.'

There was silence again, and then he said, 'My name's Caleb Hanson. Hell of a name, really. Pleased to meet you, after all this time.'

'Mine's Ruby Smith.' I watched him, waiting, but

he turned blandly upon me, innocent and full of politeness, as if it had all been a mistake. 'What do you mean,' I said, 'after all this time?'

'Why, simply that there you were in that café yesterday, and then again in the hotel last night, and then again at breakfast, and we even went on the same walk this morning it seems, and I thought I was never going to get to talk to you.'

'Yes, I suppose that's true.'

'You here alone?' he asked me, and I lied in my defence, for my reaction this morning was all suspicion. There was no need to tell, no need to meet him. One does not have to make a connection with anybody if one does not want to. Travelling, one does not have to tell the truth. 'I've just come for a short break, I'm on a sketching holiday, England gets so full, you know.'

He looked at me and did not say, 'I have not seen you sketching but walking fast about the town, looking for something.' He was quiet for a moment, and then said, 'Yeah, it's a good place for it, I imagine. Amazing old town. Did you know that one of the French kings, one of the Louis, I forget which, there were so many, set off from here on a crusade and never came back? He sailed off down the Grau du Roi, the sea came right up close in those days. He took off, with all his army, and never came back.'

'Why? What happened?'

'Nobody knows. At least, I don't. Found a woman in Palestine, I expect, or got knocked off trying. No, I guess they were killed. All those armies going east, filled up to the eyeballs with blind faith, so damn sure they were right. All that self-righteousness

90

against heat and disease and rotten boats and the Infidel at the end of it all. I'd a vague idea of writing a long poem about it. It's been coming back to my mind since I've been here.'

'You're a poet?' It was I, now, who became the false interviewer, leading him on.

He laughed. 'Well, I'm a person who writes poetry, put it like that. I've published one slim volume, out of print as far as I know. What about you?'

'I only teach art in a school.'

'But you paint, you draw, yourself?'

'Of course. But only for myself.' Why did I nearly tell him, 'Anna's much better than me'? I shut my mouth tight.

He stared down at me, his face like a Red Indian's in its composure, with the large nose, the set of the lips. 'Who else would it be for?'

'Well, I mean, I'm not – I don't sell anything. You get published. People read what you write. Some, anyway.'

'Well,' he laughed again, more from habit I felt than mirth, 'I don't do it because I love mankind, and that's for sure. I reckon they could get on without me. You never change anybody's mind, you never move them a fraction away from their set view of what's going on. People always read things into what you say, what you write. Nobody wants to meet another mind, another intelligence. They just want a reiteration of themselves.' He finished his drink and looked at me over the rim of his glass, and I was caught for a moment in his gaze, uncomfortably, as if I were half in and half out of a room in which I had been spying. His eyebrows were raised, he expected perhaps my contradiction.

I said vaguely, 'Do they really? Yes, well, I suppose it's comforting to find one's thoughts put better by somebody else.'

'You mean, they're frightened of meeting what the other person really is. The poet, whoever it is, the person. Most people just don't want to get a look at another human being, it's embarrassing, it's alarming.'

'Yes, I suppose it is, rather.'

He said, tapping his glass with a fingernail, 'I don't think you've thought about it. You think about it.'

'All right,' I said, 'I will. But I don't think you can talk in large generalisations like that. After all, all you ever really know about is yourself.'

There seemed to be pain in his face, and anger. 'Oh, God,' he said. 'Well, I hope I manage to find out just a bit about somebody else before I die.' And there was silence again, while I listened to the echo of the desperate sadness that was in his voice. I thought: he seems to be the connection between where Anna is now and where I am now; and yet how is this? Our cards were still clutched in our hands, tight and secret, but I felt sure, that he knew, as I did, that each of us had something to tell. Our defensiveness spun a web around us as we sat there, weaving curt response and abstraction around the direct meeting of our eyes.

He said to me at last, 'Are you short-sighted?'

'Yes, a little. Why?'

'I wondered what you see. When you don't wear your glasses. I wondered why you've taken them off.'

'Partly because I can see things close up without

them. Partly because I don't look nice in them.

'Now you've taken them off,' he said, 'I can see you've got beautiful eyes. Some short-sighted people do, in a very particular way. They look kind of wide-eyed and have a mistiness about them, as if they saw a better world. When you came down the street, you must have seen the house and the people clear and sharp, the way I see them. And now, do you see them like an impressionist painting? A canvas of blurs and blobs and moving colour? Can you see me, can you see my face, or am I a blur too?'

'I can see you fairly clearly,' I told him, 'You are clearer than the rest.' I nearly told him, slipping again, that without my glasses I am helpless in a shifting world of colour, in which only the nearest objects are solid. But I protected myself. 'I must go,' I said, 'I have things I must do.'

'Shopping, you said.'

'Yes, shopping. Various things. Well, thank you for the drink.'

'Don't thank me, it was pure self-interest. Well, I'll see you again.'

'I don't know.' I stood before him and could not take my eyes from the steady gaze of his intelligence.

'Well, you can hardly help it, surely, if we're staying at the same hotel.'

'I don't know,' I said, 'I may be going.

'Where to? You've only just come.'

'I know,' I said, 'but still, I may be going.'

'Well, in that case, good-bye. Thank you for your company.' He was polite in his annoyance. I crossed the street and turned to wave at him as I stood on the corner, to show the same degree of politeness. He

waved, smiling as if he had known me for years, and
shouted, 'Don't wear yourself out!' and I shook my
head. He was already a blur, a blue shirt and a brown
head beside a red circular table; only his voice was
clear. I took my dark-lensed glasses out of my bag
and put them on instead of the ordinary ones, and
hurried away out of sight. There were still about six
hotels I had not visited, and in one of them Anna's
name would be known. I was still unaware at this
point, I think – for so we are taught to look only at
the surface of events – that anything about my search
had essentially changed. My aching legs carried me
up and down streets, across the square again, down
to the city walls, almost back to where I had begun;
I stood in shadow with my list of hotels and made
black marks against the individual names with the
stub of a pencil. In my anxiety I had started to be-
have like a policeman. I looked up, suspicious, when
somebody entered or left one of the hotels, I ques-
tioned the concierges and the porters and left them
staring after me as I went, discomforted at my persistence. The last hotel on my list was the *Lion d'Or*;
it was a house in a terrace with a veranda, and a
menu pinned up outside. I stopped to read the menu,
and the words began to work upon me as pornography upon the sexually deprived; I stood there
salivating, weak at the knees, my stomach crying out
for gratification; and had read only as far as the salad
when I saw the blue shirt of the American in the foyer,
the fall of his bleached brown hair unmistakable
above it. He was standing at the desk and ringing for
attention, his hand raised to a small white button on
the wall. I mounted the steps, came in through the
94

half-open door and stood silently behind him, breathing in controlled shallow gasps, so that he should not
turn and see me. The concierge came in her knitted
mauve dress and propped the soft bulk of her bosom
upon the desk. 'Monsieur?'

'Bonjour, Madame.' He was slow, he was careful,
he must have produced these phrases so many times;
he spoke as if at an elocution lesson, fearing to be
misunderstood or taken lightly. 'Can you tell me
please if there is a young lady here by the name of
Miss Anna Parrish?'

'No, Monsieur.' She was sure.

'The young lady has not been here? During the
last few days?'

'No, Monsieur. An English lady? No, Monsieur, I
am certain. The only visitors this week from England
were a couple, middle-aged. They left yesterday.'

He inclined his head, coming closer to follow her
words, feeling the shape of her words, I imagined, as
if he were blind.

'I am sorry, Monsieur, that I cannot help you. And
now, Madame?' She looked at me across him, and he
turned and saw me, and his face was quite blank
with surprise, so that I could surmise nothing.

'Hello,' I said, 'Would you like to get me some
lunch? They have snails on the menu, and there are
quite a few things I want to ask you.'

Snails, frogs' legs, odd little cheeses wrapped in
leaves, the non-taste of white unsalted butter, the
different tastes in wine; they have the same preoccupations, they glance earnestly out at the world
across tables spread with food, through walls dotted

with paintings and streets crammed with buildings; there is that look – how can I say what it is, exactly – asking perhaps for something not in their experience, waiting to be told of something else. Emancipated women, surely travelling in Europe, seeking an ever more refined version of what they have been used to from birth, yet at the same time demanding something more. Something they can take home with them, perhaps, something like a rough piece of rock to finger in the hand; for all these meals are digested and gone, the finest taste upon the palate momentary only, all the paintings must hang for ever on those immemorial walls and not be moved. People do buy buildings and take them home, they purchase the Tower Bridge and set it up in the back yard; but they have missed something, they surely have to go on looking. Perhaps these two have taken home their thousands of souvenirs, their little pieces of the common experience, perhaps their rooms in London are littered, lined with stones and shells and such; perhaps they are still here because it all turns to so much dust, perhaps they started looking for something else and have forgotten along the way just what it is. For what are they now, twenty-seven, twenty-eight? Pushing thirty, at a guess, even. And they still have the shy questing look of college girls, the blunt question followed by the blush, the bright round stare that demands some sort of answer. I am caught in a conspiracy of immature English women, educated, rootless, destructive, fascinating. I am paying once again for a long, elaborate and alcoholic lunch. They say you create women for yourself out of some lack, possibly left by your mother. That you fall in love with a type, made for your own destruction; and yet, no, not love, I will not use that word, for there is nothing of love in it, you are drawn rather to such and such a one of this type, to cast yourself fatally into her; I am made to think of running towards a mirage, thinking that I will swim in it, of casting myself in hallucination at last upon the burning sand. Two Englishwomen on holiday. Two friends, one trying to find the other. Why? I do not know. They do not find each other, but they both find me. Why? I was not looking for them, I was on a journey away from sexual encounters, on which I was to lick my wounds. One mother in Mississippi, one wife in New York, one ex-lover in Paris – that, one might think, would be enough. But I have to sit in a room into which walks a girl like the Mona Lisa, a girl, a woman with the face and body of a beautiful hermaphrodite, I have to entangle myself with a thoughtless English bitch in the middle of France; I have to be fool enough to hunt for her when she is gone and so find upon my trail her friend, the ugly and intelligent one of the two, I imagine, the one with all the imagination and none of the self-confidence. One supplies to the other what is needed, that is the pattern of these friendships. A man may face two girls like this and fancy himself in love, because the composite is so charming. But it is war he is in, it is strife he is entering, because couples like this are self-regarding, they attack men and eat them for dinner. Eating, the archetypal fear of man for woman, of being eaten up. Women used not to be greedy, but took dainty little mouthfuls, because of their corsets of course. Whenever I see a woman eat now, it is like watching a wolf. Freud, I expect, watched the little teeth flashing, the jaws rhythmically crushing. It is really very funny, when you come to think of it. Well, she has finished gouging out the helpless bodies of those little snails, she has mopped up all the juice with her bread and put down her implement and sits smiling at me triumphantly, the garlic butter on her lips, and since I am paying for this demolition of food, I imagine I had better set about ordering the next course.

We drank red wine and finished our meal with slices of soft goat cheese, laid on leaves, and peaches that were dusty and rough to the lips and spurted warm red juices. Our exchange of words, at first built up tentatively over mutual suspicion, grew and quickened as we ate and drank; I thought, how the lulling of the senses with food and wine eases our minds, so that we can no longer remember what we were looking for. He would not try snails, but sat looking puritanical and crumbling bread. At last, when I had finished my peach, I found myself sitting in silence, all the questions that had come to mind suddenly confused and pointless.

He sat back, unwrapping a new packet of cigarettes as soon as he had taken his last mouthful, dropping the cellophane among the abandoned pieces of peach and cheese and bread upon his plate. He said, "She's an old friend of yours then?'

'Yes, we've known each other since we were children. We were at school together. She used to live next door.'

'I see. So you must know each other pretty well.'

98

I was confused, not knowing what I should answer. I said, 'Well, yes, I suppose so. I suppose I know Anna as well as I know anybody. But actually I hardly know her at all, come to think of it. I mean, where is she?'

He sat opposite me, a person who had appeared in Anna's life, apart from me. 'Well, I thought you could help me more than I could you,' he said. 'You see, when she took off, I was pretty sure she'd come on to Aigues-Mortes, since she'd mentioned she was meeting a girl-friend here. So I came.'

'I suppose it's quite funny, really,' I said. 'But I can't help feeling a little worried, all the same.'

'Funny? Is it?'

'Funny-peculiar,' I told him, 'not ha-ha. You know.'

'Oh.'

'Sorry,' I said.

'And are you angry, too? That she's not here after all?'

'I suppose I am, rather.'

'Nobody likes being taken for a ride,' he said. I did not tell him what had just occurred to me, that my anger was because I had guessed at the truth about him and Anna; for this puzzled me still. One should not expect people to be predictable.

'It's terrible, somehow, when somebody just goes off like that, when you expected them to be there,' he said.

'I know.'

'And you're left with the sensation of something unfinished. You have to go on, to find out what the end would have been. It's no good being left with just a few clues.'

'I don't know any more than you, though.' I broke
a piece of bread and moulded it into a small doughy
ball between my fingers. 'I mean, this is the end of
the line for me, too. I've no idea where she might
have gone. I suppose it is just possible that she might
be here, and we haven't found her. We both seem
to need her to be here, don't we?' I did not mean to
say this, but it was out before I could think. He
looked at me after this as if his interest were suddenly
aroused; he moved as if about to say something, but
then changed his mind. 'We certainly looked pretty
thoroughly,' he said, and smiled at me, inviting me
to mock him in the way he mocked me. 'Between us,
we must have covered about every inch.'

'Yes, like a couple of dogs on the same trail, having
a brief snarl at each other every time we came within
sniffing distance.' We both laughed, long and helplessly, in a release of tension, and others in the dining-
room looked round at us and smiled and looked
away, looked at a couple sharing a joke as if we fitted
easily into their landscape. A woman at the next table
leaned over and said something quietly to her husband, with an amused glance at us; I assumed at least
that he was her husband, and she, catching my eye,
looked away, for we were young and might have
wanted privacy. Caley offered me one of his long
cigarettes and lit it for me, so that our hands were
close for a moment across the table, the flame of his
lighter flickering high and then extinct. It is an
accepted ritual, and if I smoke cigarettes it is because
I desire a share in it, the communal act.

'I suppose one should give it up, really,' Caley said.

And I said, 'Yes, but I like being surrounded by smoke. I like making it, making a screen.'

And he said, 'You like to hide, and so do I.'

Out of such things, out of the prosaic and the glib, I felt companionship grow, and our ease with each other; so that it was no longer necessary to talk all the time about Anna and explain all our actions in terms of our search for her. When we had finished eating and drunk all the wine, I found that he had paid our bill already, as if it were a matter of no importance, as if fumbling in bags and pockets and counting out francs and translating them into sterling and deciding whether it had been good value were activities that simply cluttered and clouded the clear surface of life; in the way that only Americans I have known have managed these things, it was settled. He said, 'Well, what now?' and I said, 'Well – ', unsure of demanding his company yet reluctant to resume my aloneness.

'Well, what now?' Unkind of me to leave it to her, to make her decide whether or not she is self-sufficient. She has rather a pleading look, it strikes me, as if she wants to do the right thing and is unsure what it is. We have finished at last, she stretches like a cat after a good feed, then remembers herself and is stiff and upright again, like a schoolgirl. My head aches with wine and cigarette smoke, I only want to go to sleep. I could go back to the hotel and send her off to do her shopping, which she has not done and which I do not believe exists, so that we would only have to meet again this evening, I would only have to pass her table at dinner, on my way out as she sits

down, and say something friendly and disappear for
ever. We are both, after all, travellers in Europe, and
that has its conventions. I make myself think of
Anna, but am too lazy, too sleepy, too drunk perhaps
to know what I should do, even to know what my
inclinations are. Life seems all at once too compli-
cated for a hot afternoon. And she, the other one,
Ruby Smith – what a name – is looking at me in
embarrassment, trying to say she is busy for the
afternoon, unable to say it; her eyes are large, nearly
black, with their distended pupils, they are somehow
hot, like a brew one might take on a winter night;
she is not wearing her glasses, and her face is defenceless without them, naked, hardly tanned yet,
dry soft skin I imagine, as if it had been dusted with
powder, as if it would be softly furred, a little rough
like the skin of that peach. She has been waiting for
me, I have been unkind in making her wait. I shake
myself awake, free from my fatal lethargy, and look
at her.

'Could we go somewhere in your car, if you're not
sick of driving? Is there anywhere special you'd like
to go?'

With relief, too fast, 'Of course,' I said, 'I'd really
like to drive to Les Saintes-Maries. Have you been
there? There's a fortified church, like a castle, and
in the crypt there is a black virgin.'

'A black virgin. Yes, I would like that.' And he
smiled at me again with that broad slow creasing of
all the lines of his face, that concentration from the
very centre of his eye, and smiled so long that I
began to blush, not knowing what he meant, not used

102

to this scrutiny, and grew hotter until my face burned
against the palms of my hands when I raised them
to cover it. He said, 'Although I've had rather a dose
of virgins, white ones anyway. I wonder if a black
virgin can blush. A black saint, a black pearl, a black
tulip. Something extraordinary about all of them,
isn't there? The miracles from among the ordinary.
Like a black blushing ruby.' He teased me and, my
cool hands upon my cheeks, I looked out at him.

'Why are you called Ruby? It's odd being called
after anything particular – a jewel, a virtue, a flower.
Think of being called Chastity, say, or Deadly Night-
shade.' We were both laughing, but it was like the
hysterical laughter of children, pushed too far in an
adult game.

'After my grandmother. God know why she was.'

'And I was called after my grandfather, and his
grandfather was probably a Bible-thumping hell-fire
preacher. So much for names.' But he said mine
again, as if it fascinated him. 'Ruby.' And when he
said it, I saw myself in the palm of his hand, a stone
that his fingers could close upon, shadowing its red
facets from the light of day; and for a moment I
could not move in my chair at the table, even though
he already stood up to go, for I knew all at once that
my freedom to go had been curtailed.

The church at Les Saintes-Maries rises like a cliff
from the ground and generations have huddled there,
safe from the sea and the invader and the hand of
temporal power. The gypsies' virgin stands in the
crypt, smooth and blunt-faced, an ancient wooden
doll, round sightless eyes carved convex. Around her
in the darkness the candles burn, high and low, and

some go out, gutter to a blackened base, some are lit newly and carry a straight yellow flame. The air is hot as wax. People stumble in the confined space, bent beneath the pressing ceiling. The stones are black after fire, sooted after centuries. I lit a candle, believing in ritual and magic, thinking of pilgrimage. Caley came and looked briefly and could not breathe, so I found him again standing at the church door, propped in the sunlight, waiting easily as if I had been to an appointment. Inside, in the dark buried heart of the church among a hundred others, my candle still burned, my pagan offering.

'Feeling better?' I ask her this, as she comes out looking so light-hearted, as surely people ought, out of churches. Most of the others come out as lugubrious as sin, and it warms me somehow that she comes light and almost dancing, straight towards me, to find me where I stand, as if she knows me so well and I always wait here for her and that is that. She smiles confidently, but as if I could be anybody, any friend of hers; there is a sort of promiscuity in such a smile; it is a smile meant for the world at large and not a particular man. I want all at once to be a particular man. Not a piece of a world she sees as good, not even a goddam poet who's going to find words to say it all,' not even the man I was yesterday, this morning, an hour or two ago. There is a quality about her that stuns me, makes me stop and gasp: what is it? Oh, words, words, elusive but necessary; honesty, that is it. She is gracefully, honestly, unashamedly herself, suddenly, this afternoon, coming out of that grimy little church; and she looks relieved, as if she

104

knows it too. To celebrate the moment, I reach for her hand through the crowd of tourists. I hold it in mine, small, warm, firm; I hold it carefully as if it were a whole live animal. We walk along, slow and casual, close together, smiling our amazement at each other. For once I have no idea what I am doing. For once, just for the record, I am happy.

And so this strange day passed, and by the end of it at least, I was forced to admit to myself that I no longer cared so much what might have happened to Anna. This could perhaps have been said by both of us, but one never knows exactly what is in the other's mind. In the evening Caley and I sat close to each other and when I remember last night it seems that we are perhaps close to protect each other from something. The picture is clear again, static in my mind; the meaning is not. Caley sits reading a newspaper, trying hard to understand the French. When Madame Devrier comes in I tell her that I would like to change my room; that any other room will do, but that in the one at the back, for some reason I cannot sleep. She looks at Caley, wondering, at his bent head, but I shake mine, glad that he had not noticed, and purse my lips as she would, to say no.

'Tiens,' she says, 'I am sorry, Mademoiselle. Perhaps you will be more comfortable in the small room at the front. I will show you. You can move your things.'

'Thank you, Madame. You are very kind.' When I return an old man is sitting beside Caley, peering at him and trying to talk, and Caley is being polite, raising his hands palm upwards and smiling, unable to understand. I am surprised at the tenderness I feel for him, as he sits there being polite to the importunate old man. The man is not the same one who sits in the corner, evening and morning, but another, also dressed in blue, with a beret, a more noisy and persistent old man. Madame Devrier lays a hand on his shoulders as she brings him a drink, and I wonder if they are related, if it is perhaps he who is the *patron*. His moustache curls grey and yellow above his glass and is wet when he has drunk. I sit down and ask him to speak slowly, for my friend does not understand French, and he smiles and turns to me and says, 'Ah, but you will understand, Mademoiselle. You speak French very well.'

Madame Devrier has gone back into the kitchen, as nobody else is waiting at the bar. I sip my glass of wine and light a cigarette and hear words drift over me, as if I slept. I am tired still, after last night and this morning and the wine at lunch and the heat at Les Saintes-Maries; tired but physically well, at peace, not receptive at the moment to anxiety.

'Didn't you hear about it, then? Didn't she tell you? Didn't Jeanne say? Oh, these things happen, I know. But it's a sad business, a sad business.'

'What is, Monsieur?' Caley has not understood, so I had better ask.

'What are you telling them, Jacques?' Madame Devrier comes back, her sleeves rolled, her hands red from peeling vegetables, and the old man says, 'Oh, just this business about the German. Cette affaire-là.' I see in her face a conflict, swiftly resolved. Her dark eyes grow larger, she is preparing to act a part. 'Oh, heavens, they won't want to hear about that.

You don't go on holiday just to be told gruesome stories, after all.' She used the word *macabre* with resonance.

'Well, Jeanne, and did the police discover anything after all that?'

'No, no. Well, there wasn't anything to discover, was there? They just keep coming in and poking about and getting in my way, asking these endless questions. But after all, a death's a death, isn't it, a corpse is a corpse, when all's said and done. No amount of questioning's going to change that.' She pursed her lips, stood there above us, musing. 'It's extraordinary, though, how difficult it is to deal with them. I remember with my late husband, I had to get his body home somehow, and the business it is getting a corpse on a train, really expensive, and no end of trouble. A dead man's even more of a liability than a live one, if you ask me. You see,' she turns to me, 'this fellow died here. A German. And nobody knew who he was, where he came from, nothing. He never spoke much. We just knew he was waiting for his wife to turn up and join him, he was sure she was coming here, and he waited long enough for her and then at last she turned up. Just in time to get him shipped home. Didn't speak a word of French, she didn't. Just turned up the morning after he died. Well, I suppose she was his wife, but how can you tell? I gave her the room number and up she went, and the door was open I suppose and there he was, dead in his bed. Quite a fit-looking fellow really, and not so old. Heart attack, the doctor thought it was. Must have got him suddenly, in his sleep.'

'You mean it was here? In this hotel?' I knew

already that it was; but then one has to say something.

'That's what I said. Day before yesterday, that's all. Bit of a shock, naturally, and not good for trade, either, if it gets about. People are superstitious. They may think they're educated and above all that, but in the end, they're superstitious. Funny, really, something like that happening right on your doorstep. It makes me feel a bit strange, I must admit.'

I glance at Caley and he is as bewildered as a deaf man trying to read her lips; he stares into her face with great concentration, but has seen no guiding clue. He looks at the old man, and the old man pats him on the hand with his veined brown paw and says, 'Drink up, son, don't look so worried. These things happen, that's life, eh?' But he has not seen that Caley is lost in the maze of language, far from the centre. He is an old man who has survived his contemporaries, laughing at the perversity of life, enjoying a drink in the evening. Jeanne Devrier smiles at me, seeing that Caley has not understood. She says, 'It's easier for women. We have to do all the dirty work, after all, bringing children into the world, sitting up with the dying, laying out the dead. We can't afford to be squeamish. But men, they're lily-livered on the whole. Take my first husband, for instance. Passed out, he did, at the first sight of a battlefield, and arrived back home to me in his coffin. Now what use is that? No, you have to be tough in this life. Women do. Men are babies, after all.' Ce sont des enfants, quand même. I look at her in confusion, amazed that she can say this, but can find no words to refute it. Caley smiles at us in all

108

his innocence; he is the man who sits beside a window and has not seen the face, pressed against the glass and then gone. His lips curl at the corners as he smiles, and I decide not to tell him, not to say. For after all, as Madame Devrier would say, when all's said and done, whatever has all this to do with us? There is a train speeding from this place towards an unknown destination, somewhere in Germany, and on it there is a dead man, laid in a coffin, the man who died in my back bedroom upstairs. But there is no need for Caley to know this.

Later that evening, he asked me, 'What was all that about?' And I replied, 'Oh, just some weird story about a man who died while on holiday. I didn't really understand it all. They have such a strong accent down here, it's like listening to a different language. I think they must have read about it in a newspaper or something,'

Caley simply said, 'Oh. I really must learn some more French. It's absurd to be here and not understand.'

'Are you in France for long?' We had moved away easily from this thing that for some reason I feared. We were back on the obvious track of getting to know each other; question and answer, measured, civilised; one tracks to and fro between external signposts, trying to find a way into an inner world.

'I've been here since March. Before that I was in London. God knows – I suppose I'll be here anyway until the winter.'

'And then you'll go back to the States?'

'No,' he said, 'I can't. I can't live there any more. But the damn thing is, I don't know whether to apply for French or British citizenship. I can't decide. Anyway, it takes so long.'

'France is good,' I said, 'There's more room in France. But there is the government.'

'The government's everywhere,' he said. 'That's why I don't know if I'm on a fool's errand. I don't want to live under any government, that's the truth of it. I don't like your government really any more than the French, and they're both on the way it seems to me to being every bit as shitty as the American.'

'Surely in England one's a bit freer?' I said vaguely, falling in line with my north-country liberal ancestors. But he was looking sceptical, screwing up his eyes, muttering, 'It's all the same thing in the end. Just degrees of freedom, doled out by an essentially controlling central party.' As I did not answer, he said more loudly, more directly to me, 'Anyway, aren't you running away from something? England can't be everything to you, or you wouldn't be here.'

'Just myself, I suppose.' I spoke after silence, after thought. 'I felt I needed waking up. One gets so stuck. You know, the rut, a terrible cliché, but still. I suppose travelling's a cliché, too. Travelling to broaden one's horizons, to find oneself, all these things one says. The whole of the western world's busy scurrying about from one end of the earth to the other, you know, hitching to India, bumming round South America, working passages this way and that. It makes my little trip round France look a bit pathetic. Oh, everything one does has been done a million times before, it's awful.' As I spoke, weariness invaded me, my mind and body drooped; it seemed

110

all at once pointless to speak to him even, pointless to explain, to try and find the right words, to put across a reasonable case. 'Oh, God,' I muttered, suddenly afraid that I would cry.

'Yes,' he said to me, his voice gentle and quite different, 'It's inevitable. But it isn't the action that matters, it's the way you do it. It isn't what you do, but who you are. You mustn't say that, you're damning the whole of mankind, you're seeing us as rats in a trap, Ruby,' We were in the street, sitting upon a bench under a plane-tree. I did not remember getting there; we must have walked and walked since we left the hotel. The dry leaves clattered against each other overhead in a warm wind up the street. He put his arm around my shoulders and pulled me against him, and said quietly, 'I may have sat like this with other people at other times. You must have done, too. It might even have been in the same street with the same tree behind us, with that same cat – there – licking its paws after eating fish. But it isn't mechanical. It's new every time. Once things become mechanical, you're dead. Don't try and get out of it easily by saying everything's a cliché and nothing means anything because it's been done before. Really. The world's diseased by a constant search for novelty. Everyone wants something new – a new trick, a new technique, the latest experiment in living. A new language. Well, the old one's bloody marvellous, I think, and I spend my time, quite a lot of it, trying to free words from being clichés. You know, I mustn't say this, because it's been said before. I mustn't go to the south of France this year because, God, how boring, everyone's been there, it's become a cliché.

I can't even make love to somebody because it's
become a cliché, I have to invent all sorts of gim-
micks and tricks and novelties to make it fun.'

I was silent, liking to hear him talk. It seemed to
allay some deep anxiety. I felt, no, it is not true; I
have never sat like this in this particular place with
this particular man; I have never sat quiescent, feeling like this. And then it struck me that he was silent,
looking at me, and that his last spoken words had
asked me if I liked him.

'Yes,' I said. His lips touched mine, so that I could
just feel the width of his mouth, dry and tentative.
Then, by some strange common consent to restraint,
we stood up and walked, with our hands joined, back
towards the hotel.

In the little hall, he faced me and said, 'Why were
you frightened about that German? Why did you not
tell me the whole story? What was it all about?'

And I shivered, still clutching his hand, 'Supersti-
tion, I suppose. It happened here, you know. Just —
oh, intimations of mortality. It can get you any time.
I don't know why, I didn't want you to have to know.'

Under the swinging yellow bulb, on that square of
carpet, we stood holding each other, our bodies fitting
closely, hardly separated by our clothes; and again
my weight of anxiety lessened, my perpetual self-
questioning died away; the story of the dead German, once told, had lost its power, for it had been
received and understood. I need no longer clutch my
fears to myself. But then Madame Devrier came
through from the bar and clicked a door shut so that
we broke apart and mounted the stairs to our separate but adjoining rooms.

112

'Good night,' I said to him.

He stood still, looking at me, and replied, 'Good night.'

And so my journey continues, and I must look differently at what I find, for Caley tells me that it matters. He does not have to say it; he is there, everything, the smallest thing, matters. A landscape of astonishing beauty opens up before us, and we are to have leisure to explore. There need be no more justifications, we do not have to tell ourselves of ends and reasons, nor motives that are respectable. The flat lands of the Rhône delta are our desert, the white roads pointing to unknown domains our oasis paths, the place to which we travel our mirage on the far horizon; we know it is not there. The roads tremble with the illusion of water, and pampas grasses shake at their sides, white hair in the slightest breeze, the home of heron and flamingo. There are horses, knee-deep in seas, white tails floating and manes streaked with mud, their ribs arched and plain, their muzzles lifted to stare towards the sky; horses and cattle; men and dogs; tourists in long boots waiting beside a corral, the wooden posts of shanties stolen from a western film; there is the sky, green as an apple, lying in a pure line along the land. On the windscreen of my car a hundred insects spatter in blood, on the radiator grasshoppers squash and tangle, as if we travel always in the opposite direction to the insect world. My vision of the vast unknown spaces of the earth is brought to me in miniature, a small part of the real wastes, yet as true. There is still the urge to leave and the uncertainty of where to go, the knowledge that we will be together, the searching for a place, for the background that will do for us; and still the isolation of the traveller who passes the homes of others, never knowing them nor hearing the words they speak. We are both strangers here, therefore free of knowledge and of obligation, both taking refuge behind the glass and metal of a moving car, both needing courage to get out of it, and pause, and begin to commit ourselves again. Beside me he sits, a person I hardly know but who persuades me in the movement of his hands and the rise and fall of his voice, and in a hundred small gestures, that he will tell me something, change the way I am. My journey, I thought, was mapped out for me; I was to follow Anna and find her, and now I have turned off from it without a thought, followed the first beckoning. I have turned down the first side road, and am lost on the beginning of another journey, and have no inkling of its end.

We hardly talk. He says, 'Will you light me a cigarette?' for he is driving my car, and I light one and pass it and exclaim, 'Look, a pink flamingo! Look, a wild herd!' and he does not look for more than a second, but keeps his eyes upon the road and smiles. We no longer speak of Anna; for in the corner of my mind, locked up like a rat in a cupboard, is still a small fear; and in the corners of his are the unknowable thirty years before we met, and the unknowable future. We start to speak to each other as if the day that we met was the first day, numbered in the new calendar of a revolution. Our words are brief, raw, tentative, because language too was changed at the revolution. We are two figures in a

114

landscape that is vast, there for a long day. The land-marks are all changeable, fluid. We tell each other at first that we are going to a certain town, to see a certain thing, and on the way we have changed our minds, our suitcases are still in the hall of the hotel where we stayed; we tell ourselves at first that we are going out only for the day, but on the way we have changed our minds; he only says, once, 'I left my poems in my suitcase,' and I say, 'When we go back I will read them; when we go back.'

We eat platefuls of rice and meat, and drink wine that has been grown in sand, we stop to look at a row of horses, chained up, and give one of them a piece of apple and ask how much it costs to ride; we stand on a piece of shore that is ashen, like the surface of the moon, where trees that have been twisted in the sea lie beached, and pyramids of salt cut geometry into the sky. We draw up as the sky turns green at the horizon, outside a hotel that stands all alone in the countryside, and when we get out of the car our shadows are long and thin and black and the heat in the air has gone, the flies gather and there are mos-quitoes under the trees in clouds. I look across at Caley, for we have spent the whole day together in a dream, and now suddenly the day is over, it will soon be dark, my consciousness has returned and makes me wonder what he thinks and what will happen next. We stand beside my dusty car, and I feel that some sudden lack of confidence in him brings me back to consciousness, to practicality.

'What are we doing here?' I asked him, as if we had not spoken all day.

He looked at me as if shocked by unease out of his
115

reverie. 'We'll have dinner,' he said.

'I haven't got any money. Only about three francs, anyway, my travellers' cheques are in my suitcase.'

'It's all right, I've got some.' He pulled his wallet out of the back pocket of his jeans and glanced through a packet of notes. 'I've got plenty. Don't worry.'

'I don't know where we are. Aren't we miles from Aigues-Mortes?'

'Not all that far. The Camargue isn't that big. We've been going round in circles.'

'Oh.'

He held out his hand. 'Shall we go in then?'

I did not take it, but walked beside him, meekly, towards' the darkened façade of the restaurant. I thought of my dusty feet in sandals, my short wrinkled skirt, my arms and legs bare, scratched, bitten by mosquitoes, my hair a tangled black mop from walking in that hot wind from the land; I thought of going into that lighted place, where waiters bustled about taking the orders, where people were calmly sitting down to dinner. At the door he turned, hesitating to go in. I saw a woman in a red flowered dress poised in the bar, draped upon a stool, sipping a long drink, and the flash in gloom beyond of a waiter's white shirt.

'What's the matter?'

I ask her this, but I am asking it of myself. The car stopped, we got out, everything was suddenly still. What am I doing? Is it I who take the initiative? Am I initiating yet another appalling mistake? And why do they never say no, no I will not come with

116

you, no, I am busy, no, I am waiting for somebody else? We will go in and sit down and I shall buy yet another long meal, I shall get pleasantly drunk once again, and then what – shall we return to our hotel in Aigues-Mortes, say good night politely once again, she wondering why did he not, am I ugly, am I not as good as the other, I wondering, am I a coward, have I missed the point? Or shall we say – a room, a double room for the night, please monsieur, no we have no suitcases, no, not even a toothbrush – and make love, or vent upon each other the accumulated frustrations of our separate lives, because in our society this is the thing one does next, before parting, as elementary as shaking hands? And faces averted from each other upon the pillow, our separate thoughts will go on, boring as railroads running into the future – she, he was not as good as X or Y, he came too soon, he did not think of me, he is remembering somebody else as he lies there, but still, but still, it was better than nothing, one must be grateful for what one gets; I, burning with my awareness of all this, remembering others as she thinks, is it me or is it women, why do I fail in this test society supplies for us, the one you read about in all the magazines, why must I be judged and not simply accepted, or am I wrong and simply paranoiac, is it she after all who is frigid? And parting, forgetting, never having known more than each other's names and bodies, with a few factual details thrown in, we will stumble away from each other, never knowing why.

'*You aren't thinking about me. What are you thinking about?*'

'*Nothing.*'

'I'm not ready for you yet – no. Just a minute –' Why must this conversation run through my head now? God damn it, damn her. *Anna, cool and naked upon the bed. There was a hard window ledge beneath my elbows. I sprang away from her, turned my face to the warm wind of the night. She made me feel to the depths, burn with my fault.* No. We must eat and then go back. I cannot risk the whole charade again.

'Caley.' Which of them is it now? My sunburn still stings my cheeks and I ache with thirst.

'We needn't eat, need we? I'm not really hungry, honestly. We could go back. We had a lot at lunch. I'd be quite happy to go back.'

'Really?'

'Yes. I'd quite like to go to bed early and read.'

'What are you reading?'

'*Resurrection.* Though I've hardly had a chance since I left England, somehow. I've only got to the court room scene, you know, when he recognises her as the girl he seduced.'

Resurrection. I think of her sitting in her solitary room, puzzling perhaps over Tolstoy, holding the accumulated rancour of a bitter old man in her hand, turning the pages, finding herself denounced.

'Let's stay and have something to eat.' I am only thirty-one, I am not going to punish her with the lifetime's mounting acridity of an old man, 'Just a small supper. I'd like to know what you think of *Resurrection.* Have you read *Anna Karenina?* D'you know, he dismissed that in a few words, saying it was easy enough to write about a fashionable adulteress – ' We are through the door, she is turning to

118

me, arguing, agreeing; I see again the confidence that was in her face when she came out of the darkness of that church, the unselfconscious confiding to me of her thoughts; in a word, her trust.

When he looks like that at me across the table, there is no mistaking it. His words die away, he was in the middle of talking about a novel, telling me – his eyes are wells, dark, disturbed, into which something has been dropped. My hand lies upon the table-cloth limp as a mouse and his is warm, covering it. I can hardly turn my head from side to side, nor speak, nor have any being. He shakes his head, smiling at me. 'I have forgotten what I was going to say.' I feel a smile stretch on my face as if I slept and dreamed and waking, remembered my dream. Drinks are brought, and more food; it is once again time to eat and drink and my jaw moves like slow machinery, my fork clatters upon the plate in the silence. There is a man asking if I would prefer fruit or crème caramel; the choice is impossible, I am silent for minutes at a time. Gently, as if to an invalid, the man brings a large golden pear upon a plate, and I stare at it, thinking, it is too beautiful to eat. The man opposite me smiles at me still; and cuts a peach in half, delicately, and detaches the red stone.

In the dark upstairs a light flashes on and the room is lit with a yellow glow that makes the curtains and bedspread livid as faces beneath a street lamp. I see my face in the mirror and it is sallow, the eyes an owl's, the mouth pursed to scrutinise. Behind me, in the mirror, there is the figure of a man in a blue shirt, who is moving to and fro and carefully folding up the bedspread as if he were at home. I turn from the mirror, my fear abating, because he is so concerned to fold the bedspread right. I say, my voice strange, 'It is a horrible colour in this light,' and he says, 'We don't have to have a light,' and I say, 'I would like to read your poems, when we get back.' He has no shirt on now and his chest is sparsely furred with straight hair like a cat's, brown and silky; he has a large dark hole for a navel, very unlike mine; he turns to pull a cord that draws the curtains and stands playing with the tarnished golden tassel at the end, that reminds me of my pear. I stand there in my brief blouse and skirt, my arms crossed and my hands upon goose flesh, waiting for the world to turn and time to move on. He says, 'God, I'm tired, suddenly.' And I say, with relief and disappointment, 'Well, let's just go to sleep.' And add, to reassure him, 'I'm tired too, terribly tired.'

'Do you often sleep with people?'

'No, not often at all. Practically never, actually. Really, only ever two people seriously, that is – ' I chatter at him, I realise; suddenly I see him, standing there by the window, I hear myself putting him off with my chatter, my explanations, and he using words, questions, to defend himself. He wants something, needs something – I am all strained, thin-skinned with a new perception, I see something in his eyes, a look, that of a horse that has been beaten, that once approached, gentle and unafraid and was hit over the head, and now stands shaking, wanting to move forward, muzzle all pointed to sniff out danger, lips curled to take in the smells, to know what is happening to it. I am jolted into this entirely

120

new sensibility of a need that is not mine, that is nothing to do with me. Outside there are owls and mosquitoes and a whole dark secret night, a moon and stars and prairie, covered by galloping horses; there are other places we could go, a hundred ways in which we may separate. His fear seems to transmit itself to me, he is afraid of me and this makes me instinctively afraid myself, but it is a surface fear, there is something more, something deeper and I have to go on, move nearer, take my deliberate steps towards him; I come right up to him, closer than I have been all day, and do not recognise myself in my movements, my inspirations, he is a map over which I move, small and docile and painstaking in the darkness. One of us has flicked the switch and the light is off, the darkness kind, no perspective anywhere now, no lines and forms and spaces, past or present. I lie beside him and hear him quickly breathing, I exist only in my skin and in some hot inner place, I am both still and vibrant, silent and shouting aloud, and he, he is hands, finger-tips, a weight, a blackness, an invading point, a rocking boat upon a black sea, a flood of noise and triumph; our long day lengthens into night.

When I was nearly asleep, he half turned, his back sticky and damp towards me, and said, 'Anna? Are you? You can't be.' And when he said this, I was certain that he was already fathoms down in sleep. I said, 'I am Ruby. I am Ruby,' and there was no answer.

In bed, early in the morning, he asked me, 'What day were you born?'

'April 26th. I'm Taurus, but only just.

'No. I meant the day.'

'A Friday, I think. Why?'

'Loving and giving,' he said, 'Friday's child. Better than all the rest. Wednesday, I was born. It means I have far to go, doesn't it?'

I said, sleepy still, 'I haven't thought about that old rhyme since I was a child. Do you believe in things like that?'

'I suppose I must, since I remembered it. Anything to get one out of believing in total free will. Like believing in the stars. One has to have a few anchors, don't you think?'

'I burned a candle in that church we went to.'

'Do you believe in God then?'

'I don't know. But as you say, one has to have a few anchors. I propitiate fate, I suppose.'

'Well, is it fate that makes one meet people, or chance?'

'Oh – well, I suppose one is drawn towards people because of something in oneself.'

'But that something can make mistakes.'

'No,' I said, considering, 'I don't think so. It's just not knowing oneself that makes it look like a mistake.'

He was silent, stretched out beside me, looking up at the ceiling. This physical closeness, I thought, this peace allows one's thought, like a fine net, to draw everything towards one to be seen. His hand lay upon the sheet, tanned except for a thin band of whiter flesh upon the fourth finger. 'Are you married?' The thought at the moment held no fear; all thoughts were possible, equal as bright fishes drawn

122

up in my net.

'I was.'

'But you only took your ring off quite recently.'

'Yes. For a time it was a sort of anchor, I suppose.'

'Oh. Yes. It must be hard to make the final break.'

'It's like breaking out of a jail. The other person's just another prisoner. Inside habit, inside convention, inside the sort of images society expects.' He sighed deeply but seemed at ease, as if he did not mind speaking of it now. In spite of this feeling, I said, 'I'm sorry, I shouldn't have asked. It's nothing to do with me.' He looked surprised, raised himself on one elbow and said, 'Oh, surely it's everything to do with you. Who else can I tell? I can trust you, can't I?'

'Yes.'

'People call it love, but it's not what I mean by love, that sort of devastating attack on the other person. You know, we sit there and remember that we once said we loved each other, and that makes it worse. And every now and again we get up and claw a bit more off each other, cutting right down to the bone. Searching for some inner weakness, the final vulnerable spot. We're ruthless, like vultures. We hover round each other and watch for each other to fail. Hell, it's all in the past tense now, I'm not going back. Did you know that sixty per cent of all American marriages fail because of sexual problems? I read it in a magazine somewhere.'

I said without thinking, 'That's idiotic, I mean, sex is simply part of the whole thing, it just means you hate each other basically. Anyway, it's not only America.'

He smiled with extraordinary tenderness and relief. 'Of course. You'd see that. But most people just read the damn magazine and believe every word.'

After a little silence, I asked him, 'What does she look like, your wife? What does she do?' Since it was impossible to ask to be shown her essence.

'She writes for magazines.' He laughed, 'So you see why I'm always knocking them. She goes round having check-ups to find out why she isn't pregnant, and she takes – took – me with her. But the experts never ask her, do you love this man, or do you grind him to pulp when he enters you, do you welcome him or lie with exasperation on your face, your eyes turned up to the ceiling. They just poke about inside her and take my sperm in little bottles to be analysed. Christ, am I sick of jerking off into little bottles. She's a beautiful woman in a way. She's tall, and blond, she wears her hair in a sort of roll these days, and big glasses. A sort of frigid librarian look, recently, although she used not to be like that. She comes from Boston, from what is known in the States as a good family. Rich, with a big old house. She doesn't want me to write poetry unless I'm a big poet, with stuff in all the Sundays and people coming to take pictures round the house. She's classic. But as you see, every-thing I say turns out bitchy. You'd probably like her. You'd probably get on all right. In a way, she's like –'

'Anna?'

'Yes. Oh, God. But look, I woke up happy. Did you wake up happy?'

'Yes.'

'Do you often?'

'Usually quite happy. Not as happy as today.'

'Well, I don't usually at all. So it's a change, isn't

it?' I took him in my arms again and my hands
passed over his shoulders, over the slight roughness
of his summer tan and the few brown freckles, and
down to the soft skin where the sun had not been; we
lay quiet, heavy, silent; as if we had been thrown up
together half drowned upon the shore. When we
made love, with the sun coming through the curtains
like orange juice, and the wings of pigeons fluttering
upon our eyelids as they swooped and rose, I felt him
driving through me, drilling the earth, hunting in
savage determination for something that was not
mine, not there to give; and I hung back appalled
and afraid, the tears from my eyes blotted upon his
shoulder, my body shaking with apprehension; the
curtains swung and light came up and blinded me,
and the breeze brought them down again so that all
that was left was the red mark of brilliance in a twilit room; the birds clattered to land on the roof and
fell again past our window, white bodies plummet-
ing, wings remote and soft. Striving to fly, beating
my wings to swoop and dive, I was earthbound,
chained within myself. Almost before he had finished
I was saying, 'I'm sorry,' and when he fell a dead
weight upon me in exhaustion, my words were carried on by the movement of the curtains, the vacil-
lating bright light, the wings that rose and fell in the
morning outside, carried to echo in silence. He said
nothing, hardly moved. But I could feel the wetness
of tears upon my chest, and my own flowed again as
if a stream had been released from behind concrete,
flooding after a storm. As our tears flowed separately,
I felt the weight of human experience behind such
encounters as ours, the dead hand of old habits and

old fears, the strain of past relationships. We met, wounded, in a strange country, crossed it through an effort of our own will, following our own ways, and faced each other in a strange room, rented for the night, with all our pain and knowledge pushed on one side; and expected a miracle. And like medieval pilgrims, we found always what we had not looked for, the miracle was not like other miracles, but was entirely ours and it was not always the one we would have welcomed.

Coming away from the hotel, along the wide eroded way we had come, we were stopped by a policeman who leapt suddenly from behind a hedge and waved his arm; or so it seemed. This conversation, or exchange of words rather, remains in my mind; it is a piece of the whole; Caley, afterwards, said it was simply another example of government bureaucracy, the spread of fascism, the categorisation of the individual, but I could not say what it was to me; a vague threat, only, a fertiliser to my dormant fear, bringing the seed of life. In my mind I examine it again.

'Where are you going, Monsieur?'

'To Aigues-Mortes.'

'Why?'

'I am staying there. I am a tourist. Why,' insolently, in English, 'Is Aigues-Mortes out of bounds this morning?'

The policeman's face closes with anger. I remember what I have heard about the French police, and touch Caley's arm, to beg him not to be rude. I feel myself all English suddenly, sure that if I can only

126

speak, my charm, my background, my harmless liberal ease, my island dwelling ancestors will calm the man and allow us to go on. But both ignore me, recognising in each other the old enemy, each one drawn to his target.

'Is this your car, Monsieur?'

'No, it belongs to the lady.'

'Why are you driving it? Have you a licence to drive it? What is the number plate please?'

'I am driving it because I am a gentleman from the southern states of America, where I was taught to treat ladies like ladies and drive their cars for them. No, I do not have a licence. Do you want us to change seats in the name of democracy?'

'That is not necessary. What is your name, your address, please, your reason for travelling in France?'

'Caleb Hanson.' He pulls a card from his wallet, on which somebody has drawn, in black ink, naked cherubs and bunches of grapes around the inscription of his name and his address in New York. The man peers, glares at him. 'My reason for travelling in France – ah – well, to see the beauty of your country, to take a holiday, to write verse, in short to have fun.'

The policeman writes in his book. I wonder if 's'amuser' is the last item on his list. He looks up, deciding to move on to me.

'This is your car, Madame?'

'Yes.'

'And what is your name please?'

'Ruby Smith, twenty-nine Edith Grove, London S.W.3, travelling in France for pleasure.' I see Caley's smile from the corner of my eye.

'And this car is licensed? You have your papers please?' I hand them, silently. It is so ridiculous that I give them away graciously. He flicks through, not understanding I think. And hands them back.

'You were exceeding the speed limit, Monsieur.'

'No, I was not.'

'Monsieur, you were exceeding the speed limit. I have a witness. You will kindly admit that you were exceeding the speed limit.' Another one has appeared, armoured in blue and white. 'No,' says Caley, 'I was not exceeding the speed limit.'

I see their faces, crammed square against the window. 'We could have been just a bit above it, I suppose,' I say tentatively. The first policeman, the tall one with the moustache and weak blue eyes, writes again in his book. 'Very well,' he says, addressing me, 'Will you drive on, please. Will you accept a caution. Please remember that we have your particulars.' And accelerating, crunching on the gravel at the side of the road, his mouth pressed tight shut, Caley pulls the car away from them and we are free, they only small blue figures, impotent on the verge a hundred yards away.

'What a ridiculous scene,' I say, or something like that.

'Bastards. You should never give in.'

'If I hadn't, we'd still be there, swopping names and addresses.'

'Too bad, we were in the right, weren't we? It's just a load of bureaucratic horse-shit, and you have to fight it.'

'Caley, it doesn't matter that much, surely. They were bored, I expect, they had nothing better to do.

Policemen everywhere are pretty thick, no resources, you know. They can't think of anything except stopping people for speeding. Poor things, what a job, anyway.'

And the last thing he says is 'You don't know anything about it.' So my silence lasts nearly back to Aigues-Mortes. I sit and fight with the irrational feeling that rises in me like a germ, I tell myself that it is nothing; but I see again the anger suppressed in Caley's face, making him vulnerable. We seem to continue on our way, frail as castaways in a coracle that will be smashed easily against the nearest rock. An hour ago I was enclosed with Caley in a world we discovered, we were together in our isolation; now I see the world out there and it is threatening us. There are victims all around, and accusers. I shiver as we enter Aigues-Mortes, and the shadow of the high stone walls falls upon us; I am struck with a premonition of violence.

As we stop the car, he says suddenly, 'You know, I really want to leave this part of the country.'

'Yes?' It is not as I remembered France, here. I think of the bleached and sanded branches of the great dead trees upon the beach, the piles of salt standing in desert land and want all at once something green, something soft, with fat cattle and rain.

'Shall we go somewhere else tomorrow?' We sit in the bar of our hotel in Aigues-Mortes, and upstairs all our belongings have been moved already into the room with the rose pink covers that looks out upon the street.

'Yes. Where shall we go?'

'We'll decide tomorrow. Okay?'

'Yes, we'll decide tomorrow.'

We finish our drinks, and Madame Devrier stands behind the bar still, wiping glasses, preparing for the evening's crowd. There is a slight wind rising from the sea, and the plastic strips outside tap against the closed bar door. Madame Devrier says, 'Did you see the Camargue, then? It's beautiful, isn't it? Did you see the wild horses? Did you swim in the sea?' And we smile and make the polite noises of tourists who have enjoyed their time spent in a strange place yet cannot find words to sum it up. We tell here that we are going early to bed and she nods with the tact of a hotel keeper who is used to the comings and goings and sudden couplings of the transitory world that passes through her doors. Upstairs in the room with the pink bedspread Caley stretches himself on the bed full length and murmurs, 'God, I feel exhausted.'

I stand by the window and push the shutters open and feel the stir of wind in my hair, cool upon my face. Down in the street a couple of men cross towards the hotel and I hear the bar door open and shut and the plastic curtain beat its tattoo, and a car comes down beneath me, its lights swing up the wall, dip and disappear. Along the street, in the town square, there is music from a juke box; I hear the remote familiar song that plays in London and New York, coming in wafts upon the changing breeze, an aimless dancing beat to which nobody is dancing. In the whole town there are only a few people moving about outside; it is, this evening, a fragile colony built upon the edge of the sea, walled against invasion yet ready to be swept away; an outpost; the relic of a civilisation that is passing in the night. I think of

130

the king's ships moving out to sea, never to return, of the tideless beaches from which nothing is swept away, nothing cleansed, but where objects lie still until they rot and mingle with the sand and the wind blows paper along and the bleached bones of trees lie dry above the water-line. I want the wind to rise and the sea to be driven up its banks like the live seas on the east coast of England, to invade the walled cities and sweep the beaches clear and recede leaving everything changed; this place is too old, too change-less, dry upon its mud banks with the wind playing only lightly around its towers, the fears and crimes of generations lying like stacks of rotting paper in a box, never disturbed, only augmented daily. I know that we have come and will go without leaving a mark, as thousands have been and gone. Nomads move through cities and leave only their debris, for they carry their world with them in the tents and vans of an ordered, moving life; but we have come with nothing and will leave with nothing, taking to the road again simply because it is easier than to stay. We search for claims upon us, for reasons to stay and reasons to change; and the cities turn their blank walls to us, wedding parties form and disperse in the streets, men in cafés turn their heads and look away again, households greet us with vague interest and we run from what we see, flee to the farthest points of the land and stand upon the shore looking out to sea; and know that while a wave fingers the beaches, never farther, never nearer, we will grow old and die.

'Will you get up a minute, and I'll take the cover off.' Caley rolls from the bed and between us we fold the bedspread, observing a ritual. This much has already solidified between us. We fold it neatly, in smaller and smaller squares, and put it on top of the wardrobe, and turn down the sheet and pull the curtain tight; as if by method we will find a home, as if in a tidy bedroom with everything arranged we may make predictions for the future. But the strange chaos of nakedness and desire makes us leap together, making the gestures of familiarity futile; we are not familiar, not used to each other, the folding and the tidiness are not yet for us; a tangle of sheets on a hotel bed, coffee cups left for another to wash once we are away, these are our props; the sight of each other and the touch is still overpowering, the act of love a journey in which all is terror and discovery and delight.

'I thought I was too tired.' Caley laughs, shaken with laughter, lying upon me so that I too shake and stream with tears and mirth and relief and fear, so that nothing is what it seems, feeling is simply a jolting to the shudder of the present. I fall asleep with the light still staring in my eyes, the roughness of his hair under my chin, the long weight of his body pinning me there, and my hands flung out to the edges of the bed. At some point he must have got up and switched the light off and covered me with the sheet and come back to curl around me in sleep.

But I awoke in darkness and felt his back to me, the long ridge of the spine against my side, still and curved as an ammonite in rock. And I lay with my eyes wide and the darkness close against them, soft and shapeless so that I saw and recognised nothing but was fixed remorselessly to the centre of my mind,

132

where all was fear. Looking back upon the moment, I recognise the possibility, the existence in us all, of madness. I tried to think; to remember the name of the hotel, the day of the week, Caley's surname, the road we were on; but my mind was numb, useless, could only present to me again and again, like a machine, the sensations of the dream from which I had awoken. I lay and felt a hand out of the past trap me, the movement of time lost for ever, a dreadful repetition all I would ever know.

'What did you dream? Tell me.' This time the questioner could only be myself. I think of Caley; but he sleeps on beside me, caught in his own world. I think of Anna, who knows me well; but her voice is gone, it is not she who asks me.

'I dreamed of death.' That is easily admitted.

'Whose death? What kind of death?' The questioner insists, I must think it all through.

'My own. I was dying of cancer. I was being eaten away, quite quickly. I looked down and saw my own flesh rotting. I knew I had a very short time left in the world, I saw that it was infinitely precious; but it was too late, too late to do anything about it, too late to move away. My limbs, my genitals were being gnawed away. My hair fell out, and somebody provided me with a hideous blond wig, so that I looked like a doll, and the wind blew, I was on the beach where the dead trees lie, the wind blew from the sea and my wig blew off, and I was bald. I had a pressing sense of something that must be done, but could not remember what it was. I still cannot remember. What is it? What can save me?'

'This was a dream, remember. You have awakened

from it now.'

'But the sense of it stays with me. Why was it so frightening?'

'Well, why was it so frightening?'

'I don't know. Death is frightening.'

'Is it really? Do you really think so?'

'No.'

'Well, what else was frightening?'

'The rotting away. The pressure of time.'

'You are afraid of rotting away.'

'Yes.'

'And why did you dream that dream just now? Why does it remain with you, frightening you?'

'Because I am happy. Because I don't want to be reminded. I don't want this happiness to go.'

'You are afraid of it going.'

'Yes.'

'Why should it?'

'Because it always does.'

'Because you don't deserve it?'

'Yes.'

'Who does deserve it? Who gets it and deserves it?'

'Somebody else, not me.'

'Somebody else tells you they deserve it, and you don't?'

'Yes.'

'Who is that?'

'Everybody else. Not me.'

'But somebody in particular?'

'Yes, perhaps.'

'Well, who? Admit it.'

'Anna.'

'Has Anna ever really implied that, or said it?'
'No.'
'So you made it up.'
'Yes.'
'But it nevertheless seems true?'
'Yes.'
'Do you know why?'
'No.'

I remember I lay exhausted, a part of me relieved, a part puzzled. At last I rolled close to Caley, as if he were my only hope, and shook him until he awoke, for it was too much to be alone any more.

'What is it? What's the matter?' He drew away from me, retreating into sleep, leaving his hand heavy upon my belly.

'Caley. Caley, please. Don't go back to sleep. I had a dream.'

'Honey, Ruby,' he was heavy with sleep, his words buzzing ineffectually, his hands upon me like weights. 'Go to sleep, honey. It's all right.'

'Hold me,' I begged him, a prisoner in this world while he trembled on the edge of unconsciousness. 'Please.'

He dragged himself up like a great whale from the deep, and wrapped his arms around me, the hair of his body tickling me, the bristles of his beard pricking my shoulder, and I lay enfolded, eyes wide open still to plumb the darkness, and was gradually soothed by the heavy regularity of his breathing as he slept; and eventually I slept too, almost against my will; as if I knew a scene awaited me to which I must return.

In the morning, the air was fresh, summer renewed by the breeze from the sea, and we went early along the coast to a place where we could bathe; and crossed a hot road and bright sand, carrying our bathing things and a bottle of wine, bread, cheese and cigarettes, down to a place behind a sandhill; and the sea was glittering blue. There were several other couples, lounging together, walking hand in hand into the shallows, sharing a picnic, men and women happy and half-naked, knees and elbows dusted with sand, hair damp like seaweed, the music of tiny transistors and the bags of possessions to unite each pair. In such a place and in such a light, it was easy to forget for the moment the fears that had still held me upon waking, to throw off the feeling that something would find me out in my precarious happiness with Caley and drag me back to where I was before. It was easy to watch him skim small stones across the surface of the sea and to lie back under the caressing heat beside him, so that our bodies made shallow indentations in the sand, easy to agree that soon we would rouse ourselves to go elsewhere, that when the sun set and time moved on again, we would be gone.

It was in the early afternoon that we stirred again and felt our tongues thick with the after-taste of wine, our heads hot, limbs stiff and coated with salt and sand. The paper bags we had brought lay between us, spilling crumbs and tiny pieces of cheese, and there were cigarette ends squashed in the sand, an empty bottle, the stones of peaches around us. It had seemed, I remember, a very normal way to be spending a day. 'Look,' I told myself, 'Couples every-

136

where. Enjoyment easy. No threats to frighten them.'

Caley said, 'What about a shower, and bed?'

And my dry tongue and lips fumbled to answer him; when we stood up and began to move up the beach, the sky struck at us with its brilliance, sand streamed through our parched nostrils and was gritty in our mouths, we clung to each other and each step dragged us down in sand, the bag and bottle were impossible weights, our clothes like chains, the world paining us with its intensity. I thought of water and cool linen, saw red patterns leaping in the sky.

Caley said, 'Christ, I feel terrible.' And I nodded, with a slow and clumsy movement, a puppet jerking upon a wooden stage. At the hotel he said, 'God, make me good, but not yet!' and I was laughing avoiding the pain in my head, when Madame Devrier signed to him to come across to the desk. 'You go on up, honey,' he said to me, 'I'll see what she wants.'

But I lingered upon the stairs, for I felt I might fall without him, and clutched the banister, peering down into the bar. I heard Madame Devrier say in French, 'There is a telegram, Monsieur. It arrived this morning,' and Caley say, puzzled, 'A telegram? For me?'

'It is in English.'

'Oh, it's for Ruby, not me. For Mademoiselle Smith, it says.'

'I cannot understand English.'

He was taking it from her, it had been opened already, it was a tattered piece of yellowish paper over which all the hotel staff had already pored. 'It looks pretty garbled,' he was saying, 'but I'll take it up to her. Je le prends.' He always remembered only

too late that people could not understand him.
'Merci, Madame.'

'Telegram for you,' he said, upon the stairs, and I took it and stared at it, focusing with difficulty, seeing nothing intelligible. 'What is it?' I asked him.

'Telegram for you. God, you really are canned, aren't you?'

'Well, can you make sense of it?' I passed it to him and rubbed my hand across my eyes and saw a small stream of sand run down upon the carpet. It seemed to me that he stood there a long time without moving. 'It isn't English,' he said at last. I pulled it away from him, stared again, and said, 'Well, it isn't French.'

'Well, what the hell language is it then?'

'It's no language. It's a mixture. Wait a minute, the first part looks like an address, Lot, that's a department, that's where the painting school was. The first word must be the name of a village – ' I stopped and stared at him, feeling the paper tremble in my hand, the sand dry upon me and trickle steadily to the floor.

Caley said, 'It's from your friend, isn't it?' I had to look again, and it was as if my fingers, independent of my brain, fiercely sorted and tried pieces of a jigsaw, forcing pieces together as a stupid child might, to make them fit, finding pictures and losing them again for lack of a single piece. Yet I could not find Anna in it anywhere. I looked at him and saw an expression on his face that was almost harsh, almost a judgment.

'Pas riche,' he said, 'What does that mean?'

'Not rich. Why? Oh – Pas riche, Parrish. Could it be? But why?'

'Well, she could have been telling some bum
138

operator her message and that's how he got her name
down. Phonetically.'

'Oh God,' I said, 'Perhaps you're right. But that's
the only bit of it that's proper French, even if it's
wrong.'

'No, look, it's clear enough what happened. All the
rest is address plus instructions given in bad French
to a telephone operator who didn't understand. Or
maybe it started off as English, who knows. But anyway, the address is where we'll find her, I guess.'

'Us? Are we going there?' I looked up at him, my
head thudding with pain as the wine I had drunk
moved like poison through my body; I could hardly
stand, but propped myself against the railings as I
looked at him, and then closed my eyes and gulped
air.

'Well, you're the one who's looking for her, aren't
you?' Caley said.

'Mind out, I'm going to be sick.' I pushed him
aside and stumbled on up the stairs, my hands
groping along the panelling and doorknobs of the
landing until they found ours. I threw the door open,
fell upon my knees and vomited at once into the
bidet. When I looked up again, Caley was standing
there, holding out a wet flannel; and I wished that
he would turn away, he who had seen me naked,
heard me cry out from my very roots, touched me
everywhere with his seeking tongue; who had stayed
chatting to me even while I crouched in a roadside
ditch to pee and had stood before me himself,
casually shooting his into the undergrowth; I wished
he would go and not see me kneeling there pale upon
the floor with the sourness in my mouth and the

139

heaving of my stomach threatening something worse; for there was in his face a reserve, an indecision now, as if he wished to turn away but had not yet discovered the resolve with which to do so.

I said, 'Oh, God, I'm sorry.'

And he said, 'It can't be helped. Here, d'you want to wash your face? I think I'll take a shower.'

'Thanks,' I said, and took the flannel, pressing its coolness into my eyes, hiding from him. But the heat of tears came again and again and I stayed there, shaking with my sobs, unable by now to tell myself that I was still very drunk and that that was why I was crying. By now, it seemed, the wine was in my veins, my heart, the centre of my brain, so that there was no standing apart and viewing it, my self as observer and observed. The collapse came from the centre and shook me to my extremities. I was sick again, and went on crying, and apart from my noise there was silence in the room. I then washed myself and put on a nightdress and got into bed. Lying there curled like a foetus with my cheek hot upon my hand, I was possessed by one thought; that Anna, in sending her incomprehensible telegram had knowingly made me the victim of a cruel joke.

This story has happened before, the thought runs. There is a precedent for all this. I have to get drunk and make myself ridiculous at this stage, this is another part of what happens. Behind the pain of my closed eyes, I see another face, that of a boy named Julian.

'Julian has invited me to the art school ball,' I am telling Anna, who is sitting by the window, making a cat's cradle of bright knitting wool between the spandrels of her long fingers.

'Julian Dobson?' Her attention wavers, is held by a point outside herself and me.

'Yes.'

'How extraordinary.'

'Why extraordinary?'

'You mean the fellow who came to tea and talked about concrete poetry?'

'Yes. Why?'

'Well, you know I'm going with Nick. Well, I said I would ages ago. And then this person Julian, well, you know I'd only met him that once, at your tea do, he came and asked me.'

'To go to the dance?'

'Yes. Isn't that odd? So I said I was going already, and as he knows Nick vaguely, they play hockey or something together, I said, why don't you ask somebody else and come in a party with us? So I suppose he asked you. What an odd coincidence, really.'

And so the light fingers rise, tilt, destroy. I am always the second chosen, never the first. 'Nick has a theory that your friend Julian's really a queer,' she tells me, days later, as we prepare to go out, 'But I'm sure you'd have noticed. Anyway I suppose he can hardly ask another man to go to a dance, even if it is the art school.' We laugh, my sound blending with hers. I always laugh, to cover the silence. Her wit releases me from the duty of taking myself at all seriously, so that I move on, unaware. How is it, I wonder, that I have not seen all this before, that I may hold these scenes, these words so clearly in my mind, and not make sense of them at all?

When I awoke, Caley was there, saying, 'Sweetheart? You sure got yourself tanked up. I'll get you a tomato juice, shall I? How do you feel?'

And I sat up, suddenly relieved of all my pain and nausea, as if an abscess had been lanced; and said, 'I feel okay. What time is it? Shall we go down and have some dinner?' The telegram lay still anchored by the ashtray on the table near the window, its yellow ends flapping in the breeze; but for the time, neither of us mentioned it again.

I said to Caley, as we spread the map between us, 'It's a lovely piece of country. I came down that way, through the Lot valley.'

'Hmmm, I know it a bit. Great fields of sweet corn that nobody eats. They say it's only fit for cattle.'

'Whereas barbarians like you eat it all the time.' I tried to lighten my own spirits, to make him laugh, but he was not listening but tracing roads on the map with his finger. It had been so short a time, enough for us to feel a little familiarity with each other's bodies, to know the things we liked, even to create a few jokes, a few games between ourselves; but not enough for us to have found short cuts into each other's minds. I felt tired with the stress, longing for the relaxation that some promise of a future must give. The thought emerged, was subdued, recurred again; that what I wanted was to live with him, to stop travelling and end this worried vigilance over my own mind. The image of a house came to me, a country house somewhere like Howard's and Jeannie's, where we would grow things and be alone. But now he was taking me, in my car, to find Anna, who would be the third person, or who would even take my place. I

142

saw her look up and greet us, as if she had been expecting us to arrive just at that moment, and extend hands to make us all equals, all friends. I knew that my anger would then remain burning slowly inside me, never to be expressed, because her gaiety, her equanimity forbade it.

'I think we could just about do it in a day,' Caley said, 'if we made an early start.'

'Why don't we take it easy? Why don't we spend a night on the way? It seems a pity to rush.'

'But she'll be waiting for you,' he said in surprise. 'She might need more money or something. That cable might have meant anything. Besides, nobody sends a wire unless there's something urgent.'

'Anna does,' I said, 'She's always doing things like that. Taking taxis to go miles. She just likes doing the dramatic thing. She likes mystifying people.'

I heard my hostility, but he was not listening. 'Yes,' he said, 'I gathered that. But underneath I think she's really insecure.'

'Rubbish,' I said, 'She's the most self-assured person I know. She's tremendously good at being alone. Just sometimes she fancies seeing someone on the spur of the moment, so she sends them a telegram and tells them to come. Or rings them up in the middle of the night or something.'

'Or doesn't fancy seeing them, and walks out in the middle of the night.'

'Exactly.'

'Well doesn't that suggest some degree of insecurity?'

'It just looks like selfishness to me,' I said. This time he looked at me with surprise, having heard my defiance. There was great pain in the knowledge that Anna had treated Caley in the way she had treated so many men, in the way that she treated me at times, now I saw it – as a commodity.

Caley frowned and took my hand, turning it over in his. 'It's rather a conservative way of looking at things,' he said. 'There's always a reason behind these things. It's no good telling a neurotic to snap out of it.'

'Oh, hell, stop lecturing me, you sound like a text-book on pop psychology.'

'What's the matter?'

'Oh, how can you be so stupid?' I began to cry, tears coming easily; and he sat and watched me and did not hurry to my comfort.

'We'll stop a night on the way, if you like,' he said, 'It'd be less tiring. But couldn't you tell me – I mean, what is it about that girl?' He moved closer; crumpling the map upon the bed between us, he put a hand upon my shoulder and looked me in the face. I sat, tears streaming. 'Is it that I met her first? Are you afraid about that?'

'No – not really.'

'Are you sure? Because there's no need, you know.'

'No – ' I shook my head, wiped my tears, denying myself the comfort of trusting him. 'No, it's all right. But you want to find her too, don't you? It's not just that I'm supposed to be looking for her. I mean, you are too, aren't you?'

He said, 'No, I just think I ought to find her.' And I was, and am, sure that he lied to me as I lied to him, because we were afraid. 'You needn't worry about me,' he said. 'It was a complete balls-up from

144

beginning to end, her and me. I've certainly no wish to go mixing myself up in all that again.' And he looked away. I thought, perhaps when one is very old, one comes beyond all this; and what barriers there are, what obstacles along the way.

'I'm sorry,' I said, 'And I'm sorry to cry all the time. I don't know why I cry so much. I always have. It's nothing, it's just like people get hay fever or something.'

'You must have an allergy to feeling miserable,' he said. 'You want to cry, you go right ahead. I wish I could sometimes. It's just my upbringing. I often envy people who can cry.'

'Does your wife?' I mentioned her without thinking and wished it unsaid.

'Nope. Hardly ever. She internalises it all and it goes sour inside. Like me. We were just too sick for words.'

'Oh.'

'Ruby,' he said, 'don't bother about her, don't sweat about either of them, please. Can't one just start again, forget all the past, scrap it, wake up one day and start afresh?'

I told him, 'I don't know. There seems to be something in me which prevents it. I want to, but I can't. Oh, it'd be nice to spend another day just with you, before we –'

'And night,' he said, smiling at me over his hands.

'And night.'

'Sure it'd be nice. Well, let's cheer up, and what we'll do is, we'll stop off in a hotel some place and have a really good time.' But there was a hollowness in his tone, a forced quality to his words. 'A really good time.' I nearly said to him, 'Caley, let's stay here, please.' But some grain of reserve, of pride in me prevented it; I would not plead with him nor let him see my fear.

And so, we ring each other round with words and conjure images from the past to scare ourselves, until the rooms are full of ghosts and the air around thick with the meanings of words, and we strive for simplicity until even the simplicity of the body is covered with our striving, so that there is no simple language nor clear picture; with each gesture we throw up clouds, we stir the water, hiding our own faces; in the pools into which we look there is no clear image to stare back at us, for the ripples we have made chase across, distorting it. Behind us and before us move insubstantial figures with changing faces; Anna; his wife; the children we might have; the people we might become; the figures we may create or destroy as we move on, feeling only with our finger-tips as we pass the message of crude surfaces. We look at maps, plotting journeys, ignoring the paths of our true feelings, and veil our eyes when we look at each other. My lover has soft long hair that I can touch, and freckles on his shoulders under the tan where the sun has been, and a scar running across the palm of his left hand; I could see him walking in a crowd of hundreds, know that slight sway, that uneven hunch of the shoulders; I would know even the bones of his wrists, sleeves lying lightly upon them as he drives the car; yet in his mind he is following a trail which is unknown to me, sniffing up a scent which for me has no meaning. He chooses a place where we

146

shall stay the night, looks up with his slow thoroughness a cheap hotel in the Michelin Guide, tells me that we must buy some petrol – gasoline – and another can of oil.

'Your car sure eats up the gas,' I tell her, putting myself in charge. This is crazy, going off on that girl's trail. I can see she's miserable about it; then why do I do it? She cries, and I want to cry too, laying my head down upon the softness of her brown arms, as she lays her head. Strange to want to be another person, just for a moment; odd to want to know exactly what it's like. But you can't get near someone while you're not being honest with them, and I can't be honest until I know. I must know, I must find out. People don't just get up and leave for no reason. It's her and Nadine, the both of them. Things can happen to one just once too often. Patterns repeat, and you're a fool if you don't ask why. And yet I can't tell her, not yet. Not until it's all come clear.

In the garage he leans upon the bonnet of the car and smiles at everybody and waves his hands about, and when the mechanic brings the oil and the bonnet is up, he peers into the engine and communicates with the man in a language that is neither French nor English but that of a car freemasonry, as if this were his car. I stand apart in the gloom of the garage and the men hurry to and fro around me in their blue stained overalls. My old Citroën commands all the attention, like a valuable horse grown feeble, hands stroking the metal, the tap of instruments in the right places.

Caley is saying, like an American, what an old car.

Ah yes, the mechanic is saying, she *is* good, she is solid, they do not make cars like this any more. One must look after her.

And I, the owner, stand apart and listen gratefully to the language of technicians, for I am the one who must mount and ride away.

Caley turns to me. 'Do you know what the French for upper cylinder lubricant is?' I do not, in spite of my French conversation, but the mechanic has understood, and rushes back with a little pointed can and carefully inserts the drops as if this were heroin. I think of the garages I have entered all over France, where I was received respectfully but with bewilderment; this then was what they liked, this was what was right, a man leaning upon the bonnet, in control, a woman standing back, her handbag clutched against her legs, in all ignorance. That was why the man in Vire screwed up his face in scepticism when I disagreed with him over the tyre pressures, and why the hotel keepers paused and stared as I pulled up the bonnet in the mornings and examined the stick for oil. They close the bonnet now and smack the old horse with affection, and send us on our way; the door is opened for me and I get in beside the driver and there are waves and thanks all round.

'V.I.P. treatment,' Caley says, backing round a corner to turn the car. His hands are high upon the wheel, fingers spread, the white of concealed flesh beside the tan, his eyes peer close to the mirror, and when he turns his head to look out of the window his neck is taut above his shirt, he is all concentration and in this way completely beautiful. I think, watch-
148

ing him, that only men and hunting animals achieve this concentration. I am supposed to be watching the traffic on the road, and instead I am watching him; but he is unaware, while a *camion* comes down the road before us, and the Citroën jumps under the clutch, that I am there at all.

'Yes,' I say when we are on the road, 'It's marvellous having a French car here. Everyone knows what to do. At home, nobody has a clue. They just don't want to know.'

'Well, in the States a car like this would have been junked years ago, it's crazy.' He is guiding the car through the traffic on to the main road; we are going through Arles and up through the mountains where there are chestnut-trees dripping with nuts, and sanatoria for those with weak lungs hidden in the forests. He is enjoying it, he is at one with my car, treating it with care, and I am at last only a passenger.

'It's amazing,' he tells me, 'you driving all this way alone.'

'Why amazing?'

'You seem to need looking after. You don't even know what kind of oil you need.'

'Everybody likes being looked after,' I say, 'but you don't always get it. So you have to be self-sufficient. I've got quite good at it.'

'It's a shame,' he says, 'a hell of a shame.'

'What is?'

'Nothing. Just a passing thought. Are there any of those grapes left in the dashboard?'

I feed him grapes, one by one, and he swallows them pips and all, and each time I feel the warm

149

greediness of his lips upon my fingers, pursed and stained with juice. There is only the stalk left, with the mutilated ends and the blobs of grape upon them, and I roll down my window and throw it out.

'What else is there?' Caley says. 'Will you feed me something else?'

'Chocolate? Bread?'

'Chocolate, please, in very small pieces.' I smile my happiness at the way we extend our sensual pleasures; and he pecks the pieces up from my hand gently, and I am reminded of the warm mouths of horses on an outstretched palm. We chew in silence, and I light two cigarettes and put one between his lips, in a gesture that still seems somehow hackneyed, like smoking in bed. We are together here, enclosed in the moving car, safe it seems from danger; for the only dangers of the road are so well known, so tabulated, compared with the subtlety of arrows poised in unknown places. I do not want to stop, to risk the challenge of encounters, and he I think senses this, for he says after a while, 'It's good, isn't it? I can see the charm of being the Flying Dutchman if you can have a lady on board.'

'Yes, it's good. I want it to go on.' I mean more than I have said, and am afraid suddenly of letting this happen.

'Do you have to go back to England?' It is the first time we have mentioned any future, even in negative terms. I know for the first time too the terror of being passive and yet committed, desperate and yet deprived of will.

'I'm supposed to go back for the beginning of term. That's at the beginning of September.'

150

'Oh, well, we've got time, we don't have to think about that yet.'

'Caley, what happens when we find Anna? What will we do then?' At last it is out, and it has haunted my mind all morning. I sit tense, waiting for his reply. He is impassive, a profile turned against the road, and at this moment there is a tricky corner to negotiate, a van backing out into the road just before it. 'Stupid bastard,' Caley says, 'Why the hell he can't look – ' he gives a long blast on the horn, his palm pressed down on the hooter, so that the man driving the van shoots his arm into the air and we see as we pass his angry face, open-mouthed in dumb insult against the windscreen.

'Fucking dangerous,' Caley says, and I see that he is easily angered by the slight follies of others, that he is arrogant and noisy when in the right. Driving cars, I think, like making love, forces the human spirit out into the open all things come to the surface in anger, as in tenderness and desire. 'What? Oh, I guess we just do the next thing, whatever that is.' My mouth is open already to protest, to ask another question, but I realise that in this casuistry he is asking for my trust, my silence; and I resolve to ask no more.

We drive up through the forests of chestnut-trees in the late afternoon, and the road is steep, bending its way uphill, the old car is hot with effort, Caley silent at the wheel. I peer from my window, alert to see when the road is clear, guiding him past great wheezing *camions* that hang upon the slopes like caterpillars upon a wall, that might let go and fall back and crush us utterly. It has started to rain, the first rain since I landed, and the windscreen wipers drag to and fro with a small sound, pushing away drops, clearing a tiny space through which we see our way. The journey has narrowed to a struggle uphill, to an inability to see clearly, to a silent effort just to go on; the wide horizons I knew, the blue unending skies and flat roads are shrunk to a valley hooded with trees, dark with rain, where cliffs overhang the road. I have grown to hate this road and am afraid; Caley's knuckles are spread wide, white knobs upon his hands, and he leans forward, peering, urging an aged machine to carry us on. We stop for a moment and pour the remains of a bottle of Evian water into the radiator and stand dismayed, for this is the last water we have. Caley says, 'If there isn't a gas station soon, we'll have to pee in it.' We stand back and gulp the air and the rain, turning our faces to the narrow sky, and without speaking get back into the car, and hear the engine turn over again, and go on. There are no people, no houses, no petrol stations, no hoardings to tell us of familiarity. I tell myself that this is France, that it is small and men may cross it easily, but I am not convinced. I say to myself that Caley has driven from Los Angeles to the eastern seaboard of America, that this is nothing; but I see his fatigue and his impatience. At last, we come out upon an open plain, where there is heather, and blue flowers grow, and a brown river disappears among rocks, and there are houses; I roll the window down and fill my lungs with the damp air.

'I hate mountains,' I can say now, for we have come across them. 'I hate those dark wet valleys. If I had T.B. in one of those sanatoria, I'd just want to die.'

That was the last thing I said. 'I hate mountains. I'd just want to die.'

But he has stopped the car suddenly, I am cut off in mid-thought; he shouts, 'Get out, quick, get out, we're on fire,' and I am in the road before I know it, staring stupidly, rain streaming in my face, my hair across my eyes in a wet veil, and smoke and flames coming from the bonnet. 'Run!' he cries to me, 'Run, get right away!' and I see him through smoke clutching a rag from the dashboard, standing back helpless before the gush of smoke that rises black in the rain, and I run shouting towards the house that is nearest, waving my arms and shouting in the rain, and there is a man coming towards me out of nowhere, his face all puckered up. 'Water, water, please, my car is on fire!' There are people suddenly, men and women running from the scattered houses, and some have bowls of water, one a fire extinguisher, and I have no idea who they are; but stand back helpless in the road and turn and know that in a second the explosion will come and the fire and smoke balloon, engulfing all, curling black and violent as I have seen in films, that the roar of igniting petrol will deafen me and then there will be only burnt metal sticking up and the body of my lover like a torch dancing in death; I am unable to move, I stand and stare and feel the rain pouring down my skin inside my clothes, pouring down my face. 'Caley,' I am crying, 'Come away, come away!' I can no longer see him, there are so many people, they dart among the piles of smoke, and the old car crouches like a beast done to death, a beast tormented. 'Caley,' I am shouting, 'Caley, and even his name is strange in my mouth, for men everywhere burn and are seen in flames; but then somebody is taking my arm and a woman's voice says, 'You will get so wet, your clothes will be ruined.' I turn and see the worried face of an old woman who wears a mackintosh hood. She says, 'You will catch a cold.' I cannot understand what she says, I look down at my clothes, and when words emerge from my mouth they are a torrent of nonsense, neither French nor English but syllables I do not recognise. 'Come inside,' she is telling me in French, 'Come inside. It will be all right.' I follow her and find myself outside a house; and as I go I see the car which was so far away, and only a small trickle of smoke is coming from it now, and there are no more flames. There is a great patch upon the bonnet, like an oil painting, and there are men crowding around it arguing. One of them, his shirt sticking to him so that I see his body whole and well, unmarked, is Caley. His face is black and his arms are streaked with dirt. He is still holding a cloth in one hand, and has a small red fire extinguisher in the other. I stumble past, following the woman, as if an accident has happened in which I have no part, and I look at the car covertly, as one might glance at a corpse. I see Caley turn, his eyes upon me, his mouth stretched in a smile of relief. 'There's a garage down the road,' he says. 'We're going to roll her down. I'll be with you in a few minutes.'

And I pass like a stranger into the strange house and stand in a small living-room where there are pot plants, and a table laid, and a television in a corner. I am shaking, and hear my teeth rattle in my head;

154

I feel them loose with my tongue and think that in a moment they will all fall out. I sit upon the chair that is offered and nurse the nausea that rises, and see my hands shake. 'I'll make some coffee,' the woman tells me, and I nod but cannot speak, for the words in my mind are meaningless. She is talking on and on, telling me what happened. I sit still and think that I do not care for anything but Caley's life, that I will make any sacrifice to preserve it, and that somehow he is alive. The world is full of burning wreckage and in it, raw as a phoenix, Caley and I are still alive. I sip my coffee and look at photographs of grandchildren and try to remember how to say in French 'I may want to be sick.' But the coffee soothes me and I become quieter and am aware only of Caley's absence, for he has gone down the road with the other men, to fix the car, while I sit here, the woman waiting. I tell the old lady eventually, for conversation, 'I was sure it would explode. I never thought it might go again.'

'Of course,' she says indignantly, 'you must have been terrified, what an appalling experience. I was terrified out of my wits, the first thing I knew of it was hearing my husband shout, "Marthe, quick, there is a car on fire outside!" – a car on fire, I rushed to look out, I rushed to give him the extinguisher; and what luck that we had it, he is a carpenter you see, my husband – look, you see the worksheds out there, that big barn – so we always have one handy because of the wood. But oh, *mon Dieu*, I never expected to see such a sight on my own doorstep! What an experience! I thought, if it explodes, then our house will certainly catch fire too. And, do you know,

155

a car did explode just a bit farther down this road, only last spring, with three children in the back, too, the whole family burned alive. Burned alive. They hadn't the time to get out, you see. He was driving them back from a football match, he was a footballer. You know what that is, you have it in England?'

'Yes, yes. But the whole family was *burned*?' I am feeling sick again and think that in a moment I must ask for the lavatory. My mind strikes angrily back at this extra burden she imposes, the knowledge of a whole family burned alive, the necessity to rush away and be sick in a stranger's house.

'Terrible,' she is saying, with some satisfaction; but I cannot blame her, for at least it was not Caley and me and our children. I share with her, at the moment, the superstitious awe of those who have been saved. I tell her that I am sorry we caught fire outside her house, that I am glad it was out in time, and she accepts my apology. She turns on the television and we sit and sip our coffee and I remember that my cigarettes are still in the car. Before us, on the flickering bluish screen, there is a boat-race going on, with a hysterical commentator unable to draw breath. I lean back and watch the men struggling with their oars, the flesh on their faces drawn back with effort like that of racehorses, the water pulled apart by the passage of the boats, the land passing in a dark strip; and the man's voice flows over me, reassuring in its assertion of triviality. When Caley comes back with the lady's husband, I am calmer; they come in like workmates and pull off their wet clothes and the lady rubs them both with towels, as if they were father and son, Caley slim beside the great shoulders

156

and spreading belly of the carpenter, Caley evenly brown whereas the other is tanned deeply to the neck and has a body white as a baby's. The screen still flickers blue light, and there is something beautiful in the way they stand there beside it to be dried, raised arms unearthly, shadowed armpits dark, and then pull jerseys on over their heads and sit with their wet hair ruffled, to drink their coffee.

'Well,' the older man says, 'It looks as if they should fix it by tomorrow anyway.'

I cannot believe it. I turn to Caley and our eyes meet in pure surprise, as if we met after a shipwreck on the same island shore.

He says, 'There's a magician of a guy down there. A Portuguese guy who's fixing it for us. I had a hell of a time trying to tell him what happened, but luckily we had a lot of witnesses.'

I think of the miles of sodden forest just behind us, the roads where only rabbits and foxes move, where there are no humans and no garages. I feel that I hardly dare touch him yet, nor look at him when I speak.

He says, though, 'Thank God it didn't happen any earlier, huh?' and I have to translate it into French for the couple who sit beside us, who lean forward with their hands upon their knees to catch what we say. They shake their hands up and down and exclaim, raising their eyebrows, telling us emphatically that we had a lucky escape. The old man runs his hands through short grey hair so that it stands straight up on end and says to his wife, 'Are you going to give us something to drink, then?' and passes round a crumpled packet of untipped Gauloises. We smoke, the little bits of tobacco coming away in our mouths, Caley pulling an unconscious face of dislike. The woman brings Ricard from the cupboard and sets tall glasses before us, and we sit there, quiet, sipping the drink that sends a shudder through us with its bitterness. Outside the rain pours steadily, filling the gutter, gushing in a stream to the ground; the stalks of grass prick up through standing water, and still the sky is dark. I tremble, holding my drink; and hear the couple invite us to spend the night with them, so that we can collect the car to-morrow; I am powerless as a sick child between its parents, grateful to be put to bed.

The man says, 'Your husband will be able to go down first thing and see how they are getting on.' I wonder if Caley has noticed, but cannot tell. His eyes are closed with tiredness already and he holds his glass tight, as if it were a standard to be held aloft. And so we have soup and wine and a dish of eggs and herbs, a salad, some cheese and an apple each, and we go to bed in the chill spare room where wedding groups look down at us from the walls, dark rows of serious faces, a moustached groom and a bride with a mole on her cheek, stiff with the future that has just been handed to them. I stare at them as I undress, for Caley is in bed already, his shoulders hunched against the light; and I see the procession of children, of grandchildren, the proliferation of weddings, the white sea of flowers abandoned upon the church steps when the crowds have gone, the bed in which blood and tears and secrets are all mingled, in which Caley and I are to sleep.

I looked long at the face of the girl with the mole,
158

whose children I had seen in the albums downstairs, and caught her dark impassive stare before I climbed in beside my lover in the big stiff linen bed. It was then that he rolled towards me and took me shivering in his arms and said, 'Ruby, honey, don't ever, ever leave me.' And I promised that, whatever happened, I would not.

It was a coincidence, the man in the garage told us: petrol had been leaking from the tank and at the same time the metal arm that held the bonnet open had been left dangling, so that it touched an electric wire and a spark had been made; what should have been happening inside the engine, Caley explained to me, had been happening outside it, so that we carried with us an illicit source of energy, a bastard fusing of power. The mechanic at Aigues-Mortes must have bent the little arm carelessly, while Caley leaned against the car and I stood back, not watching. It had to be sawed away, and then when the leak was stopped, we would be safe. To climb back into the car that morning was like mounting a crippled horse whose needs we had ignored. We drove away very slowly and saw the rain drops still dripping from the trees, the ground still drenched with rain and mist rising like steam. I had before me in the glove pocket the little red fire extinguisher that we had bought from the carpenter, as if with this we could give ourselves protection, as if in all this world of uncertainty the same pattern would ever be repeated, the falling star go back into the sky and strike again.

There is a river running past the village, coming in

over a weir and falling in thick grey skeins, knotting
in the pool beneath, deep at the bathing place and
moving faster as it curls away past the last houses,
faster and away to the far sea it runs beneath a cliff of
limestone where bushes grow wild and trees jut
above the water, their roots torn out, it brushes the
low branches horizontal where the forest grows close
to the shore; steep-banked in shadow it pulls away,
moving the stray twigs midstream, tugging debris
from the sides as though it eats away the land. There
are notices, relics of the time that there was a hydro-
electric plant; but the government has closed the
plant long ago and the notices are old and unread,
stuck crooked into the ground like announcements of
no-man's-land, sucked by the soft mud. Tethered to
the shore are boats, fishing-boats; and in the shallows
men wait for carp or bream, immobile over their rods
amid the August flies. Above the small space where
people sometimes bathe and children potter on the
pebbles, two diving boards jut from the stone wall,
high and stiff above the water. The sky is poised
above the valley, kept out by the cliffs and the high
trees way up on the skyline; when it rains, the clouds
perch upon the cliffs and the water moves faster,
thicker, and is the colour of pale jade and quite
opaque. But it has not yet rained, and all around men
sigh in exhaustion over their crops, the water from
the irrigation jets falls ceaselessly in rainbows, pat-
terning the dust of the dry roads. There are geese in
the fields, fat hens and mottled ducks with strange
eyes; in the fields, maize and grapes, marrows and
tomatoes, the green tobacco leaves, the flower of the
courgette, the whiskered ears of wheat and barley;

in the gardens, nasturtiums, geraniums, basil and thyme; in the farmyards, cats sleek with milk and hunting; in the cowbyres, cows with smooth broad backs, munching the corn; it is rich, this land, fat with produce stacked in granaries and barns with the generosity of the earth and the work of men's hands. The river runs through it, thick and grey at the valley's edge; a grain, a twig dropped into its stream is gone at once, carried away, and no trace of it or its loss is there. Here, nothing need be guarded, nothing counted. The rain and sun have brought, the river carries away.

Cars sometimes park around the little patch of green grass in the centre of the village and visitors stay for an hour or so and then leave. For sightseers there is nothing that a glance at the château, a dip in the river cannot satisfy. The gourmet wants his food ready cooked, not growing upon a stem, the photographer needs a clear outline, a dramatic landscape punched upon the sky. Here the land is gentle and the river flows away and green apples ripen slowly upon a tree. One would have to stay a long time, to watch the apples grow and ripen and fall, to taste the sharp green of their juice.

Several times since she had been here, Anna thought that the roof of a parked car shining in the sun might be Ruby's, that a figure on the road, a figure on the beach might be Ruby herself; but then she realised that Ruby did not, could not know that she was here. There were times when one ought by telepathy to be able to create a presence, to summon another to one's side, times when the mechanics of letter and telephone and explanation should be dis-

161

pensable. She walked daily down to the little beach and threw a few sticks into the river to watch them drawn away, and sat in the hotel bar over a glass of wine, and wearing a broad straw hat sketched the stacked houses on the village street; and thought occasionally, it would be nice to see her. But in the evenings, when great moths with the heads of skulls hung upon the wall, and crickets sang in the maize fields and in the crevices of the house, and under the lamps sat brown toads, their mouths agape for flies, she was peaceful, alone.

A man came to the village, a Frenchman for a week-end's fishing. He leaned brown veined arms upon the bar and ordered aperitifs for them both, and sat at breakfast watching her across the room. His eyes were grey, flecked with darkness, and he had a moustache like a bandit's, a mouth small and precise beneath it, pink as a child's. She knew, looking at his mouth, that this time she would not answer but would turn away, going back to her canvases and her paperback books, so that what he pursued in her would remain illusion.

'Vous êtes très belle.' She inclined her head, accepting it, and the lamplight showed him the smooth crown of her head, neatly parted. He must stay there, hanging like the night moths upon the wall, and his voice must remain level in admiration, his eyes dark with deference, not passion.

'Why will you not come to me?' he was asking, morning and evening, with a politeness and patience born of his own security.

And she was bowing her head, telling him, 'It is all illusion. I know now that this is true. I am at rest,

162

and I will not be disturbed.

But in the French language they played with each other, and skirted round the subject so that neither was the question asked nor the answer necessary. It would last just long enough to flatter each just sufficiently, for both to go away in a day or two, content.

'You are sensitive,' she told him, to keep him where he was. 'You are delicate and understanding. Anglo-Saxon men are so crude.'

And he told her, pleased, 'Les anglais, ils ne savent pas faire l'amour. One must have subtlety and feeling.'

'Les Américains non plus,' she reassured him; and he sat back, relieved, and ordered some more wine.

'Ah, les Américains.' His tone was weary with disgust, he played contemptuously with his glass, tipping it to and fro. She wondered, with a look into his hard grey eyes, if he were the cat and she the mouse; if he had watched her cross France, taking her chances, and knew of her escape from the American's bed and saw, with a single glance at her, why she was here. She quietened him with compliments and her own suspicion grew. It would be easier if Ruby were here, to play, as she always had, the willing foil; with Ruby she could be herself without fear of censure from outside, for Ruby would laugh and play the fool and lighten the stage on which they moved. A man who met them together would move towards her and yet include Ruby; so that she would be safe.

'I have a friend coming to meet me here,' she told the Frenchman, watching him.

'A man?'

'No, a woman.'

'One would never see two French women travelling together,' he said.

She said, 'It is because they have no independence,'
and looked at him again covertly, to be sure she was
not mocked.

'Well,' he said, 'Unfortunately on Monday I must
go. La fin des vacances, you know.'

'You have a wife waiting for you?'

'Of course.'

He was, after this, more sure of her, a shade more
contemptuous. He said with a touch of anger, 'You
are so fine, so intelligent.' She knew that she had been
discarded. On the last evening he bought her brandy
at the bar and they sat outside at a little table and
saw the toads come out and crouch in the light,
facing the whitewashed wall where the insects crept
and buzzed. The toads moved like old men, bandy-
legged and absorbed as they clambered over obstacles; and every few seconds a sharp tongue flick-
ered, impaling a fly or a bug; so that watching them
was like seeing a jerking old film. He sighed and said
to Anna, 'I do not understand why you come to a
place like this.'

'Well, why do you?' She was at once defensive.

'For fishing, of course. It is my hobby.'

'Well, I paint and draw. That is my hobby. In fact,
it is what I do for a living.'

He was still puzzled. 'Yes, I saw what you were
drawing this morning. It was quite good. But why
here? I mean, there is no night life, no company, no
gaiety.'

'You mean, it's all right for a man to come to a
place like this because he feels like it, but it's not all

164

right for a woman?'

'If you like. You are so definite, so strong. I don't understand why you wait here.'

'Wait? I'm not waiting. I'm having a holiday.'

'You said you were waiting for your friend.'

'All right,' she said, angry enough now to risk it, because tomorrow he would be gone, 'I'll tell you. What it started as was hiding from someone. A man I left.'

'Ah,' he said, interested, 'your husband?'

'No, I'm not married. A man I met. An American.'

'Ah, the one who was not good making love? That American?'

'It wasn't true,' she said, 'What I told you. At any rate, it doesn't apply to any one person. It was a generalisation.'

'You are so intellectual. What I think is, when a woman makes a generalisation like that, there is a particular man who inspires it.'

'It could be a defence,' she said, and added deliberately, 'like your despising English women.'

'Ah,' he blinked, and pretended to bow before her, and her dislike of him increased, 'but I do not despise English women. They are mysteries to me, desirable mysteries. All women are mysterious, but English women the most mysterious.'

'One only sees what one wants to see.' She thought, saying this in French, that it had a good, sharp, epigrammatic quality. It was a universal statement, and it put her in control.

'True. But tell me about this man, this American.'

'There is nothing to tell. I met him, we had an affair for a very short time, and then I left him.'

'You left him? Why was that?'

'Is that the part you find most interesting?' She thought, and then said, 'Well, because he was a sadist.' She sat back, watching his face, pleased at her effect.

At last he said, 'The Marquis de Sade was a Frenchman. I find it hard to believe that an American could emulate him.'

'Well, there are degrees, after all. You are so arrogant. You seem to assume that the French are best at everything.'

'You do not like arrogance in a man?'

'No.'

He leaned towards her, 'I think you are lying, Anna. I think you like arrogance, I think you even like cruelty.'

'Don't be so ridiculous. You don't know me.'

'Well,' he said, 'I have been talking to you, watching you for three days now. One does notice things about a person. One is forced to be particularly observant about a woman as beautiful as you are. You are not like de Sade's women, then? You are not a masochist?'

'No,' she said, 'I certainly am not. I'm perfectly sane.'

'But one cannot be sane alone,' he said to her, and sipped the last of his brandy, 'any more than one can be mad alone. To make love, it takes two, to make pain it takes two, to make madness it takes two, to make harmony it takes two. So, you make a man cruel by being a willing victim, and you make a person leave you by pursuing him, and you make one thing happen by willing the opposite. That is what

166

I think.'

She sat back at the table, her fingers cold and drumming a pattern of sound, and stared past him into the darkness to where glow-worms moved in the hedgerow opposite and clouds of insects were like smoke rising around the light. She thought, 'Any philosophical remark sounds better in French'; and said to him, 'Whenever I meet a Frenchman I get lectured about the meaning of life.'

'Am I boring you? I am sorry. I thought that was what was on your mind.'

'I'd prefer to talk about something else. Could we have another drink, d'you think?'

'Another cognac? Of course. But first, if we are changing the subject, I would like to ask you something.'

'Yes?'

'Would you like to kiss me now? To make friends? To heal whatever I have said to hurt you?'

'You can if you like,' she said, and held up her face to him with that same passivity with which she had faced boys at teenage dances, when to be kissed was a social necessity. He held his pink lips to hers and fluttered his tongue inside her mouth, and she thought of the cold tongues of the toads, picking up flies, and withdrew as soon as it was polite to do so.

In the morning she stood at the hotel desk early and asked to send a telegram, looking around her to make sure that the Frenchman was not coming downstairs to discover her. She stood waiting, with a coin for the telephone in her hand, turning it round so that it winked in the sun. A man brushed against her in the narrowness of the passageway, coming from the kitchen with his jugfuls of hot milk, moving sideways like a tango dancer, his hands for trays. He had often brought her plates of food and stood back to ask if she was enjoying herself, if she would like some more wine; she knew that he was called Antoine and that he was younger than she, and now she knew that his brushing against her was deliberate, that he would pass her again, returning to fetch some forgotten cup or plate and would brush her again as he went. His hair was combed forward in a smooth cap, he had long legs and big feet and puzzled lines between his eyes, and since he wore the jacket of a waiter, she could dismiss him. When he returned, hurrying with another order for breakfast, she decided to stop him and, putting out a hand, said to him in French, 'Would you please be more careful. There is no need to knock against people like that.'

He stared at her and then said, 'Je m'excuse, Madame,' and swung away into the kitchen. She kept the hostility in his blue eyes, in which she had read that his clumsiness was unintentional, that he was in a hurry with a job of work to do; that he had seen her as nothing more than a shape, an object standing in his way; he had called her Madame and looked at her coldly. When he brought her dinner that evening, he would be a little more aloof and would hold out the wine list without a word.

The concierge came to the desk, her powdered face wrinkled in the sunlight, and she showed Anna how to use the telephone and gave her the jeton in exchange for her coin. Anna heard the muffled voice of the operator and repeated her message into the warm black plastic hole, trying not to speak too
168

loudly in case the fisherman might hear; her words
flew off upon a life of their own, to make sense or not;
the operator seeemd satisfied; bewildered, wanting
to retract something, she set down the receiver. 'I
think a friend will be coming to join me,' she told
the concierge, 'I wonder if you will have a room free,
perhaps for tomorrow night?'

'Bien sûr, Mademoiselle.' The concierge, whose
name she did not know, knew exactly which rooms
she had and who was in them, and when each would
be leaving. Her eyes, heavy-lidded, ringed with blue,
stared past Anna as she absorbed the morning,
motionless as a cow at a gate with the mist rising
about it. 'Of course, there will be a room.'

Anna raised a hand to her face and it smelt of
metal, and the stale breath of the telephone was in
her mouth. 'Thank you, Madame.' She crossed to the
little room in which breakfast would be served and
sat at the usual table by the window. She saw the
yellow van which brought the post draw up in the
centre of the village and women in black with aprons
wander out to meet it, the old ones waddling on
wrinkled-stockinged legs, petticoats dipping. Out
there, she thought, was the real life of the place. In
the cleaned dining-room, waiting for white jugs of
coffee and milk as one waited for them all over France,
she was cut off from what was happening. The post-
man knew each one of those women, and he was
chatting to them, teasing them, joking, holding the
packets of letters and newspapers up high, so that
they must guess, waiting with faces lifted like dogs;
and then he was pretending to cower under their
onslaughts of insult and was getting back into his van

for safety, starting it with a roar and lurching forward, a man with a face like a walnut, going on with his round.

'Coffee, Madame.' It was the young waiter, Antoine. She turned to him with an effort to appear impulsive and said, 'I'm sorry, I was unfair just now. It wasn't your fault.'

'Ça ne fait rien, Madame.' He had taken what she said, they had looked at each other, and it was too late to change it now. She had seen the hostility in his eyes for women who made a fool of one, foreign women with money to spend and books in a case upstairs. But there was something terrible about being waited upon by a young man who disliked one; she smiled at him desperately, but he retreated, his hands and eyes alert around what he carried, moving away to serve somebody else.

'Ah, may I join you?' It was Jean-Louis, the fisherman, the man who had kissed her lips last night, had actually pressed against her that hairy little moustache.

'Of course.' That was what one said; that was the French for tolerance, for acceptance and wariness at once. The ritual of coffee or a drink protected one; one sat straight backed, pouring out coffee, and smiled with an immaculate façade; and when asked questions one inclined one's head easily, replied, 'Of course.'

'I was planning to leave today,' he said, ducking his head over the cup, steam rising before his face. 'But I was thinking. I could stay on a few extra days.'

'Why?' she asked him, the hostess polite behind her barrage of cups and saucers.

170

'Well, Anna, after last night I thought you would perhaps want me to stay. I thought, we could have a little holiday together. Not here, necessarily, for one wants to avoid unpleasantness after all, you know, have a little discretion. We could go to another hotel in the valley.'

'No, thank you,' she said, 'I don't want you to stay. Besides, your wife will be expecting you.' She spoke clearly, her head raised, and he looked up in annoyance.

'Well,' he said, with more sharpness, setting down his cup, 'you are very clear in your mind.'

'Yes, absolutely clear. You must go home, and I shall stay and meet my friend and then go back to England, and that way we'll both be pleased we met each other. Otherwise, no.'

'You have no spirit, no imagination,' he grumbled, and dipped a large crust into his coffee. 'You say no before you know what it can be like.' He put his head sideways, his neck suddenly like that of a tortoise, and dropped the dripping crust into his mouth and sucked on it, then let go of the end he was holding and drew it all into his mouth as if it had been spaghetti. When he had finished there were wet blobs of bread upon his moustache. She watched him, and felt for a cigarette, knowing that she could eat no more nor even touch the cups from which others had drunk, the plates from which others had eaten. There were crumbs swimming in the remains of his coffee, and a pale brown stain spreading on the cloth.

'Well,' he said eventually, swallowing the last of it, 'in that case I shall leave after breakfast. There is no point in lingering where one is not wanted. I shall catch the morning train to Agen and by three I shall be home.'

'In the bosom of your family,' she said, literally translating it.

He jumped and looked at her in confusion and looked away, muttering, 'What is this about breasts?'

'Nothing,' she said, 'Just an English saying. One in the hand is worth two in the bush. Call me when you're going, and I'll come and see you off. Are you taking a taxi to the station?'

'You have a car, could you not take me perhaps?'

'No,' she told him, speaking as if to a child, 'I'm afraid not. You see, my fan belt's gone. I shall have to get it mended.'

And so she saw him depart in a taxi, his neat face pressed to the window, his grey eyes staring; he could no more look really sad than she could be sincere with him, but he made his moustache droop, and waved a handkerchief. She waved, thinking of wet pink lips and soggy little pieces of bread, and sighed; but turning, went back into the hotel with an extra-ordinary lightness of heart, giggling like a schoolgirl as she went.

The trees at the top of the cliff opposite were like a dark fence against the sky; she drew them quickly with thick charcoal strokes as a beginning, and began to sketch, more tentatively, the line of the disused buildings along the water's edge. It was a sublime landscape, grass tufted upon stone, the torrent of the river coming over the weir, the faces of the cliffs marked with hollows and striations. Upon the hill a little way down the river, a small romanesque church,

172

round and smooth among the spikes of wire memorials, the curls of waxen rose and violet, the sepia photographs of the dead upon the marbled monuments; above the weir, a jungle of small trees, tangled blackberry and old man's beard, nettles and elder; below her, where she sat, the mud on the shore, marked by birds' feet and the rubber boots of fishermen.

Her pencil moved rapidly, but she was dissatisfied and smudged the lines already drawn with a careless hand, and wished for the greater discipline of paint. There was no way of seeing this brilliant morning in black and white, for at each movement of her wrist, her eye dwelt upon the sudden blue of a rising dragonfly, the deep changing shades of the river, the purple shadow under pale branches on the further shore. She tore the sketch away and began again, on larger paper, promising herself that this would be the sketch for a painting, that she would go upstairs and get out her painting things and settle for a few days until the place was made her own, blocked in colours upon her inner eye, until she could mould with her hands that weir and the falling water, and the forms of the men casting their lines upon the shore. The day's mounting heat moved along her forearms so that they tingled and grew pink, and it warmed her back through the thin shirt; she sat still, her pencil laid at the side of her block, her hands immobile upon the paper, and stretched her legs before her, knowing a sudden assurance that she could do this, holding the clarity of this morning's vision in her mind and between her fingers and finally releasing it in paint, so that her brush and the thick colour would fall upon her canvas like the sun, light creating each leaf, each twig, each curl of water. Her body was tense with the promise of this to come, yet in her mind there spread a grateful relaxation of certainty; there was no need to strive, to be active, for the whole picture was inside her and would emerge slowly, uncurl like a new bracken plant, if she could be still and let it come. She said to herself, I will put all my things ready on the balcony, and then I will swim in the river until I am cool and faintly tired with it, and then I will begin to work. There was a rare, subdued excitement about moments like this, moments alone when sudden perception flooded in and controlled her, making her quiet like a woman who awaits the birth of a child. Indeed, when she was aware of it, she guessed that this was her portion of the love, the creation in life; no surrender to sensuality, no conception or birth could ever be like this, this handing over to a certainty that came from nowhere, was unbidden and always surprising, this knowledge that what she saw was the present moment, the present place, in its totality, that what she would paint was the essence of passing time and the structure, the colour of life. Later would come the frustration of eye and hand, the struggle for mastery, the confusion of being tired and of sensation growing faint, but through it all, like grace, would stay in her somewhere the knowledge that could never be identified, the certainty of white against green, of a block there and a line flowing and light falling like rain. How she had tried and tried for it, in recent years in London, and how it had eluded her, like a colour that has no name, a word

174

that has no meaning but a sound in the ear; how she
had grown old and tense in waiting, and worn out
with the effort of painting without it, working over
canvases that had no light, no life of hers in them.
Like happiness, this fulfilment she sought now crept
in on the wind only when it was unsought; like the
perfection of a summer morning, it could neither be
willed nor banished. She could sit there for thirty
years more, and grow grey in waiting, and because
there was no corner of her in which it was, no word
for it, no shape and no limitation, she could die
without ever stirring again under its sudden command. 'It' she called it to herself and knew now that
this was the only thing in her life that could be true.

And so she went slowly back up the steps and into
the darkness of the hotel, with images fixed before
her eyes, stepping languidly for this moment to be
prolonged and this pressure experienced to the full,
before she began the long and difficult release. In
her room, she let her clothes slip from her to the floor
and walked about the room looking for her bathing
suit and her towel, oblivious of her own nakedness
and of the shape of her body, unconscious now of
what the men she had known called beauty, the long
slope of white shoulder and breast veiled with hair
that slipped down free, the irrelevant familiar flesh
within which she lived. Pulling up the straps of the
black costume, she faced the mirror for a moment,
vaguely, and pushed her hair upon her head and
fastened it there with an old ribbon and saw herself
momentarily poised against the strange bulky furniture, the patterned curtains, a long white figure in a
black bathing costume, vacant, silent, the eyes

strained like a cat's eyes in darkness, to see. I am
twenty-eight, she said in her mind, I have wasted
time; I am not like other people, I am selfish and
snobbish and cold, but I am myself, I am unique;
there is a thing I can do, that allows me to be myself;
there is no need for men, for love, for friendship, for
houses and children and the charming trivia of
others' lives. For twenty-eight years I have been
evading this knowledge, acting a part, imposing upon
myself things that lie illegible, meaningless in my
mind, turning myself outwards to the gaze of others,
turning my body towards strangers, accepting the
vision of myself that they have seen, speaking hypo-
crisy because I dislike myself in their vision, lying
with my body, lying with my mind; I have denied
myself the right with which I was born, to be myself,
I have lived so long and do not even know what this
means. She turned away and began methodically to
set out her paints and an old canvas, rags and brushes
and turpentine and pencils, on a low table that could
be carried out on to the balcony, delighting in the
movement of her hands and the clarity of the message like a bell in her mind. Then she closed the door
softly, retreating on bare feet, a towel hanging from
her arm, and crossed the landing and came down the
carpeted stair and padded over the cold tiles of the
hallway and out into the morning that hummed and
shook around her and sent warmth up from her soles
and down through the top of her head and spreading
up from her open palms, from every side an affirma-
tion. There were sharp stones underfoot on the way
down the steep path to the beach, and then the softness of warmed mud, cooler to the feet as they sank,

176

and then there was the shallow water, the skein of weed, the line of cold rising up her calf, up her thigh, soaking through her bathing costume, flooding up her body so that she gasped and kicked free of the land and splashed away, numb at first and shouting a little with the cold, then relaxing, welcoming the flow of the water over skin scratched and bitten by mosquitoes, trailing her limbs through the depths as soft as weeds and turning up to the sky a face still warmed by the sun, still dry, still human. The small figures of the fishermen on the shore receded; one seemed to be waving, so she raised a dripping arm to wave back, and swam strongly against the current, upstream towards the weir. Overhead the trees were close, coming down like giants to the water's edge, rimming the sky; and beneath her the river was cold, deep in midstream, moving faster as if it were all will, all power, the raw electricity, she thought, that moves the world. And she swam and swam, delighting in it, and thought she saw the shape of the hydro-electric building grow smaller, with its cracked stone face and its tufts of weed growing, and heard more faintly the rush of the weir, saw the stones and blocks of houses, the bushes of grey, the trees with spiders' legs slip past her, swam still upstream, pushing now against the current, sure that a little effort could bring her back, flailing with open hands at the water, to stop it, to seize it, to bring back the past moment in which she was safe, to throw from her the hurrying, grasping future, the next minute, the next breath, the next mouthful of water, the next twist of the tide around her legs; but the houses were smaller still, and the sky more huge, the bushes passing like landmarks seen from a train; water rushes on carrying twigs, and broken fishing lines, and the toys that children have let slip, and turns them over in its grip without thought or differentiation, careless as elephants that move in chains through the jungle, unchanging as the patterns of clouds, until all is sucked away, all changed and smoothed and thrown up elsewhere carelessly or carried on for ever until disintegration releases it and the pieces, the broken shapes, the fragments of solid things are scattered entirely, and never come together again.

The group of men upon the beach expands and contracts. Black figures, flies upon a patch of something already rotting; arms rise like flies' wings. One of the men is dripping with water, gleaming in the sun. Others bend and straighten, others are prostrate on the ground. It is a scene that has been enacted before, the same men and the same background, where nothing is new. A car draws up on a higher piece of ground and the new sun strikes fire from cleaned glass, after the rain. Two figures get out and together they come down the beach and become part of the pattern of black movement against the dazzle of water, an agitation upon the outskirts of the crowd. The actors move back, their piece completed, and when they back away, stand solemn and waiting, there is a glimmer of white stretched between them, a shine of black wetness, a spread of hair light upon the stones. There is no breath in the still morning, but drops fall from the ends of twigs upon stones and grass, there is a plop of water even as a measure among the bushes. There are sighs and murmurs
178

from the crowd, but centrally there is no breath. At
the hub there is stillness, no heartbeat, no mist upon
the mirror from lips already cold. Slowly the figures
of the men move together again, and the slight form
from the stones is raised and droops from the outstretched arms of the bearers like a flower drenched
after rain, the long white arms falling away, the long
petals of a battered tulip from a broken stem. After
the moving crowd of men, the two figures from the
car come separately, a little way back from the rest.
The men move slowly but with confidence, now that
doubt has been removed; they have done this before,
have left their boats lying in the shallows, their lines
taut under the bite of a fish, and come away up into
the village with their burden; but the figures from
the car walk with the stumbling uncertainty of the
blind, feet groping a way across the roughness of
stones. Spread out in a long line, the group moves up
the hill and turns into the centre of the village.

I stood at the door of her room, convicted of relief.
Something had been decided now which was irrevoc-
able, something in which I could not yet see my own
part. It was only certain that Anna was dead and
that I, in that minute, that second even at which I
stood on the threshold and realised it, had been glad
of it. Now there were people milling everywhere
below me in the salon and the foyer of the hotel,
strangers all over the place looking and touching and
asking questions, shaking their heads and arguing
over the speed of the river, the safety of the beach.
There was a policeman now and a doctor and a re-
porter and a priest and there were people whose
labels I had not yet ascertained, yet who mysteri-

ously belonged in this melodrama. I felt I was not needed and so came away upstairs to Anna's room, hardly missed as an observer; I knew too, as I stood there and looked inside, that in a few moments the crowds downstairs would be here, the men's expert fingers touching and probing among her things, a version to be decided upon, a verdict to be made. It was necessary to find my own version before this could happen; for how, I thought suddenly and for the first time, can one accept the haphazard judgement of others? So I stood upon the threshold and knew that this was what I had wanted. This seed, planted years ago perhaps in the seeming innocence of childhood, had grown in my mind and burst and scattered its poison. I came to this place an hour too late, an hour I had spent with Caley making love in a bedroom that was found upon the way, and when I arrived all that I had wished for had been accomplished. I stood still and looked first down at my hands, the instruments of a faithless and jealous friend. Then I moved forward, hesitantly.

'Are you all right?' Caley asked me this once since we came up the beach, following Anna's procession like guests who have not been invited. Otherwise he was silent, distracted, his eyes clouded against my gaze. There was talk of suicide; he hovered near the centre, greedy for knowledge; this death made carrion crows of us all. I knew that somewhere in the recesses of his mind was the picture of another woman, fragile blonde nape exposed, librarian glasses falling, wrists in tepid water ineffectually sliced. Our eyes tried to look at Anna's body before it was carried away, but met guiltily and could not look or tell

180

each other anything. We were separate, remote, carrying our burdens up from the empty beach.

'I'm all right,' I told him, meaning nothing. He did not see me leave and go upstairs. The porter told me the number of her room. The crowds of investigators were not yet on my trail, for they still had to examine the evidence of Anna dead, whereas I knew her well. The door was ajar, as if she were coming back. A shutter swung, letting in light in a hard beam and I stepped forward against my own distaste for this violation of privacy. *'The worst thing, don't you think, going through someone's possessions?' 'But reading letters is worse. . . .'* Privacy was strong between us always, maintaining the mystery that makes of friendship more than self-indulgence. But now I moved forward, now that she was dead and I had wanted her so, for I felt that without a clue I could not live. I thought of Caley crouched downstairs, gleaning each fallen word from the mouths of policemen and doctors and priests, collecting the evidence to prove his own guilt, yet knew that for my part, only in her room would I find what I was looking for. The harsh beam from the morning sun fell through the half-open shutter upon a small table that was drawn across the window and on it I saw Anna's painting things laid out; the canvas and the paints, the brushes and old rags, all the tools and paraphernalia of her trade. They were dry to my touch, they were blank to me, they had not been used. I stood beside them and clutched up a dry rag in my hand and strained to see Anna's intention as she laid them out, I stood in the beam of light to warm myself; and all I knew was the thud of feet, the burr of voices

below, rising and falling, a car starting and accelerating in the road. Behind me the room was quiet, twilit, any room along the track of any journey, a place where people slept for the night and made love and quarrelled and died and left no trace. The bed was made, drawn neat under a shiny counterpane. There was a glass of water beside it with a dead fly bobbing, a novel turned face downwards, a jar of face cream, an opened box of tissues, a small piece of chocolate, a nightdress laid out that I think I borrowed once, long ago. Now there were only moments left before the steps below moved up the stairs and along the passage and came into this room, before every object was turned and scrutinised and noted for official records while the traces of Anna, the light powdering of herself upon her possessions, would be quite brushed away. I made myself calm, forced myself not to rush about like a scavenger, plundering her room; I crossed deliberately to look inside her suitcase, which lay closed beside the wardrobe. Her clothes must have been all hanging up, for it was nearly empty, with only hairpins and a small tin and a battered little book in the bottom; I swung open the wardrobe door and saw her summer dresses, her trouser suit, her leather coat and her shoes; the sight of them blurred my vision, I was about to sit down and cry for her and give up utterly, but I blinked and rubbed my head and went on. She seemed so neat, so unobtrusive now, I could not find her anywhere but only felt my memory stirred by the sight of her things, my guilt sharpened by their mere existence. It all looked so normal, the neat bed and the hanging clothes, the suitcase emptied as though she planned
182

to stay, the room left tidy in echo of a state of mind I could not yet imagine. I could find none of the signs of panic that my guilt informed me of. Like Caley I crouched, searching for my identity, looking minutely for objects that would give it to me. I turned everywhere, searching for the thing that would tell me that we had killed her, that would allow me to go away alone and be guilty for the rest of my life. Downstairs just now, our glances had met for a second, and all I could remember was the knowledge of an image destroyed. The mirrors that we held for each other, in which we loved to look, were filled each now with a face we struggled not to recognise. It would be too hard to go back and look again, or try for something else. What I wanted now was the simplicity of being accused; knowing it, I knew that so did he.

In the few moments left to me, I went back to the suitcase and got out the little book which seemed to be the last thing left in the room, and turned the cover open; and the surprise at seeing it was Caley's was only what I forced myself to feel. His writing, in a failing biro, covered the pages, and from the shapes I saw that these were poems. But I was unable, at the moment, to begin to read. My mind struggled with meanings, with implications; I came to a high wall and could not ascend it. My fingers moved fast across the pages and flipped them past as if this were a rosary and I praying for a favour; and then there was the last poem, which Caley had called 'Offerings', and then a page at the end, on which was Anna's own writing, neat and clear. *August 19th. Stolen by A. Parrish from C. Hanson. One may perhaps learn something from those one meets at the cost of a little pride.* Anna's last cryptic message to me. I read it again, and closed the book and tucked it into my pocket. Her voice sang for a moment now in my mind, her presence was vivid. I remembered her irony, her practicality, the jokes she had told, her occasional pompous seriousness. I was certain now that Anna did not want to die. Caley did not really touch her, and neither did I. She was intact, and made her own decisions. Certain of herself, she laid out her painting things, having tidied her room, and she went out for a quick swim, and that was all. She simply did not know the strength of that swollen river. And the next thought was of Caley's innocence, in spite of what he feared. I stood alone then, with the knowledge of my own violence and perfidy, until he came up behind me and was standing in the room.

I told him, 'Look,' and waved to the painting things, 'she didn't want to die.'

He did not understand. He said, 'Look, I know there are accidents but that girl could swim.'

'She was going to start painting. Look, there are her things. She had an idea, and she was going to paint.' I wanted him to touch them, for a talisman. Behind us the officials were coming up the stairs. I took out his book and held it out to him. 'Look, here are your poems. She took them. They were in the suitcase. Did you know she had them?'

'I knew I'd lost them.'

'She had them.' And I showed him the last inscription and saw in his face the faintest flicker of recognition, as of a person he had barely known.

But he said, 'It's true, there is a moment before
184

one starts on something, one lays out one's things, one walks about, has a smoke, one might even go for a swim. . . .'

'And forget about the current and the rain swelling the river.'

'Yes.'

'And you wouldn't go and kill yourself if you were just about ready to write a poem, would you?'

'No, I wouldn't. No.' He stepped back from me to let the first man pass, the hotel manager, gesturing, anxious, followed by two policemen, the local doctor with his black case and a tall man in a light macintosh. The little bedroom was suddenly crammed with people, became dark and suffocating. I tried to find Caley's arm to hold on to, but he had been pressed back against the wall, where he stood muttering. 'Je m'excuse, Monsieur. Je m'excuse,' his hands spread above the shoulders of shorter men like those of a miming actor. I too, trying to move, found myself held behind the door, its knob pressed back into my stomach; I pushed and called out, 'S'il vous plaît!' several times, and bursting free at last collided with Caley in the tiny patch left empty once they had all begun to swarm about inside the room.

'She was my friend,' I cried out to him, tears streaming at last as I saw them all, busy fingers, anonymous uncaring backs, pore over her possessions. And Caley, looking at me and taking my hand firmly in his to draw me away, said, 'Well, now you are free.'

We stood there for a moment, and I saw one of the country policemen drop Anna's paperback novel to the floor and then bend laboriously to pick it up from between trampling feet and put the pages that came loose with careful, trembling fat fingers, back into their place, and lay it upon the bedside table where it had been. He was quite a young man, and his face was flushed, he ran his hand across the back of his neck to ease a muscle, and I saw drops of sweat upon his upper lips. Then there was the hotel manager himself, quite close to me, his eyes closed for a second when he thought nobody saw, tension in the line of his shoulders dropping away with this hardly perceptible moment of relief. The man in the macintosh took it off and threw it down on the bed and as his fingers played with minute specks of dust upon the mantelpiece I saw sinews under the skin of his right arm where the shirt sleeve was rolled back twitch and spread. That man had a wife, and dinner waiting for him, and children who would ask where he had been. He was hungry, they were all hot and hungry and doing a job simply that they were used to doing. They had lives apart, they would depart from here in a few minutes and go off in different directions into different and entirely unpredictable futures. It was not us, it was not Caley and I who had brought them to life.

'Now you are free,' he had said, minutes ago.

'Yes,' I said, 'Shall we go?'

And as we left the room where Anna had been, we heard them all begin to shut up their notebooks and close drawers and pull down the tucked-up edges of bedclothes and come away, banging the doors behind them, leaving dust to settle and the shutter to swing and light to fall unseen again upon Anna's painting things, the rags and brushes and pots we had all left

186

behind, on that little table where she had put them. None of us would ever go back now. There would only be the chambermaid, later in the day, preparing the room perhaps for an unknown tenant for the night.

In holography an object can be recreated visually, by use of a laser beam. Each minute portion of the holographic plate contains the whole image. In a pure light any virtual image can be recreated, in the position in which it was originally seen.